"What does the baby feel like when he moves?"

Francesca's green gaze locked to his. In that moment there was a spark of understanding in her eyes that he needed to be part of this pregnancy. "Do you want to feel him when he moves?"

Before he could think better of it, Grady answered, "Yes."

She closed her eyes for a moment, and then laid her hand on the right side of her tummy. "You can feel him move here."

She was wearing a long-sleeved, purple maternity sweatshirt with matching knit slacks. He told himself he just wanted to feel the baby. There wouldn't be anything intimate about his touch.

But when he laid his hand where hers had been, when he could feel the heat under the material and then the flutter of movement, he knew touching her this way was *very* intimate.

Dear Reader,

Babies bring surprises—from their first smiles and steps to their unique sleeping schedules. As a newborn, the longest stretch our son slept was from 7:00 12:00 midnight. So that's when my husband and I slept the most, too!

In *Baby by Surprise,* my heroine Francesca is surprised by her pregnancy. Even more so, she is surprised by her growing feelings for the hero, Grady. When fate serves up yet another unexpected surprise and Francesca must learn to depend on Grady, her past wounds almost prevent her from falling in love. However, love is the biggest surprise of all for both of them, transforming separate lives into one union.

Baby by Surprise is the third book in THE BABY EXPERTS series. Three more books will follow in 2010. I hope you enjoy reading about these women who are truly baby experts and the men with whom they choose to spend their lives. For more about the series, visit my Web site at www.karenrosesmith.com.

All my best,

Karen Rose Smith

BABY BY
SURPRISE

KAREN ROSE SMITH

SPECIAL EDITION®

Published by Silhouette Books

America's Publisher of Contemporary Romance

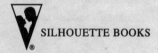

SILHOUETTE BOOKS

ISBN-13: 978-0-373-65479-6

Recycling programs for this product may not exist in your area.

BABY BY SURPRISE

Copyright © 2009 by Karen Rose Smith

Visit Silhouette Books at www.eHarlequin.com

Printed in U.S.A.

Books by Karen Rose Smith

KAREN ROSE SMITH

Award-winning and bestselling author Karen Rose Smith has seen over sixty-five novels published since 1991. Living in Pennsylvania with her husband—who was her college sweetheart—and their two cats, she has been writing full-time since the start of her career. She enjoys researching and visiting the West and Southwest where this series of books is set. Readers can receive updates on Karen's latest releases and write to her through her Web site at www.karenrosesmith.com or at P.O. Box 1545, Hanover, PA 17331.

For Suzanne and Sydney—May the future bring you
many blessings and much happiness. Love, Karen

Chapter One

Francesca Talbot barely registered the lines of wind turbines in the fields as she headed out of Sagebrush toward the hospital in Lubbock, Texas.

A wave of dizziness washed over her, leaving her suddenly weak. Over six months pregnant, she'd ignored her thirst for the past few days, attributing it to takeout food. As a neonatologist she should have known better. But she'd planned to discuss it with her doctor at her monthly appointment at the end of the week.

The road pitched and bent—

She quickly swerved back to her lane, blinking against the gray dots dancing before her eyes. The blurriness grew worse. Dizziness enveloped her. She felt bumps, a huge jerking motion that threw her against the door, then she sank into unconsciousness.

* * *

Six hours later, Francesca found herself in an unfamiliar position at the hospital where she worked—that of a patient! She tried not to panic at the diagnosis her doctor had given her—gestational diabetes. The condition would probably resolve after her pregnancy, but she had to handle her diet carefully. Everything else looked good with the baby, and…

She now knew she was having a boy.

A boy.

Grady should know.

Francesca had been talking and singing to her baby ever since she'd learned she was pregnant. She laid her hand on her rounding tummy awkwardly due to the cast on her arm. Even after more than six months, she vividly remembered her out-of-character one-night stand with Grady and, more important, her decision to experience her pregnancy on her own to give herself time to consider how Grady would fit into their child's life.

"I don't know what will happen when I call your daddy," she murmured to her son. "He told me he wanted to be involved in your life after you were born. Maybe we'll have to include him *now* just to make sure you'll have a backup."

Tears burned in her eyes. She had two very good friends, Tessa and Emily, who used to be her housemates. She hadn't called them yet, either. She was sure they'd come running to help. So why did she feel as alone as she had when she was a child, cowering in her closet to stay safe?

The phone was one stretch of the fingers too far. Francesca looped her index finger around the cord, pulled the receiver off and grabbed it. She punched in the numbers for Grady Fitzgerald's saddle shop.

To her relief he picked up himself. "Sagebrush Saddles."

His deep baritone rippled through her as it had the night they'd met. They'd attended a reception for a lawyer opening offices in Sagebrush and had bumped into each other periodically during the evening, feeling the buzz of attraction, each time having something new to talk about. With the party stuffy and crowded, Grady had invited her to the building a few doors down where he worked. They'd had a glass of wine, sat on his couch—

Erotic pictures flashed on her mental screen and she switched them off.

"Grady, it's Francesca."

He must have noticed something in her voice because he asked immediately, "What's wrong?"

"I had an…accident this morning. The baby's fine," she rushed to add. "And it's a boy. I had a sonogram."

Silence lay heavy between them for a few beats. "Are you okay?"

The concern in his voice washed over her. She hadn't expected him to ask that. She'd expected, "What caused the accident? What happens next?"

"My arm is broken, but that's not the problem. I have gestational diabetes. It caused blurry vision and dizziness. That's why I had the accident."

In the silence, Francesca pictured Grady's ruggedly

handsome face, the sweep of his black hair, the intriguing depth of his blue eyes.

"That's something I'm not too familiar with. Explain it to me," he said.

Nervous about calling him, she blurted out the medical explanation. "Pregnancy hormones produced by the placenta can block insulin. As the placenta grows larger, more hormones are produced and insulin resistance becomes greater. When the pancreas makes all the insulin it can and there still isn't enough to overcome the effect of the placenta's hormones, sugar builds up in the blood and gestational diabetes results. It can happen without much warning."

"But you and the baby are okay?"

He really was concerned. That knowledge made her heart hurt. She sucked in a big breath, seeking to escape to facts rather than her emotions. "We will be. At thirty-seven, I'm at a greater risk than someone younger. The diabetes usually clears up as soon as the baby's born."

An awkward pause settled between them, neither of them knowing quite what to say. She added, "I just thought you should know. Especially that we're having a boy. And…" This was so hard to get out. "And I guess this changed the way I'd been looking at the future… I just want to make sure our baby has another parent to rely on if need be."

She did know Grady had come from a big loving family and looked at family differently than she did. To her, family ties had only hurt.

"When are you being discharged?"

"This evening. My doctor will be making rounds around seven."

"Do you have a ride home?"

"I have friends. I haven't called them yet."

"Don't. I'll take you home."

She thought about facing him again, fighting the pull toward him, riding in his car— "Grady, that's not necessary."

"I think it is. We have a few things to discuss. I'll be there by seven unless you find you're being discharged sooner."

She'd kept away from him the past few months for more than one reason. Her last relationship had taught her she wasn't over her past. She'd chosen the wrong man. After a long-distance relationship, which had lowered her defenses, she'd moved to Lubbock to begin a life with Darren. But after he convinced her to move into his condo with him, he'd changed, becoming a man like her father.

After she'd made love with Grady, she'd been afraid to take a risk again. However, now they had to figure out how to be parents *together*. "All right. I'll see you at seven."

"Seven," he repeated, and clicked off.

Francesca took the phone from her ear and just held it in her hand. She'd learned early on fate wasn't kind. Each decision she made mattered.

Had she made the right decision in calling Grady Fitzgerald?

Grady rapped on the hospital door. He'd decided to bide his time with Francesca. Look what had happened. He'd never expected an automobile accident. But as he'd learned before, life was made up of unexpected surprises. Some nice, some not so nice. One thing he knew for sure—this baby was his main priority and he'd do whatever he had to to protect him.

A boy. Francesca had said they were having a boy.

He heard a sweet "Come in." The first night they'd met, her voice had been easy, pleasant, almost hypnotizing. She'd been so interesting. And she'd been curious about him…about his family. Her voice that night had wrapped around him like perfume, arousing him.

He pushed open the door and stepped inside the room. Francesca was standing beside the bed, dressed, only—

She was wearing a light blue maternity sweater that looked soft and lay enticingly over her. He hadn't seen her since she looked…pregnant.

"Hi, Grady." Her greeting was hesitant, her eyes searching.

"Hi, yourself. How do you feel?" His gaze went to her arm in the cast. The sleeve of her sweater came just below her elbow where the cast began. She looked pale and he was worried about her. Worried about his baby.

"I'm better now."

He couldn't keep from approaching…from standing in front of her…from touching the bruise on the side of her cheek.

She backed away from his hand and joked, "Better than my car."

The car was inconsequential. Her pregnancy wasn't. "How long are you taking off of work?"

Suddenly a physician swept into the room. He was wearing a white coat over his suit and a stethoscope hung around his neck. He was as tall as Grady, fit and good-looking.

He responded to Grady's question. "I told Francesca she should rest for a few days…at least." The man gave her a wink and then extended his hand to Grady. "I'm Jared Madison."

Francesca spoke up. "Jared, this is Grady Fitzgerald."

Jared looked from one to the other. "I'm going to give Francesca some instructions. Maybe you should step out."

"No, it's okay," Francesca told him.

Grady could sense the familiarity between the two of them.

"Jared married my former housemate, Emily," Francesca explained.

Grady felt himself relax a bit and his snap-buttoned shirt collar didn't feel quite so tight. "Is Francesca really okay?"

Jared arched a brow at Francesca, and she nodded. "She is right now. She will be if she can control her sugar. She's going to have to be more strict about her diet, exercise and get more rest."

"Would it be better if she had someone with her for a few days?" Grady asked, a plan forming in his mind.

Francesca's "That's not necessary" was overridden by Jared's "It wouldn't be a bad idea." He continued. "We don't want her getting dizzy again and falling…or worse. Maybe Emily or Tessa could stay with you."

"They have kids," Francesca protested.

"She can stay with *me*," Grady insisted without thinking twice about the decision he'd just made.

Silence fell over the room.

Finally, Francesca responded, "I'm not going to impose like that, Grady."

"You won't be imposing. There's nobody there but me and a few horses. Your friends have their responsibilities. My employees in the saddle shop can work whether I'm there or not."

"The two of you should discuss this," Jared said, obviously feeling the tension between them. "I'll send in one of the aides with the paperwork to get you discharged. My receptionist will make you an appointment with the diabetes specialist to go over diet and any questions you might have."

Then Madison put his hand on Francesca's shoulder and gave it a comforting squeeze. "You already have your next appointment set up with me. I'll see you through this, Francesca. You'll have a successful labor and delivery."

"I wanted Emily to be my midwife," she protested.

"I know you did. But she's only taking on low-risk pregnancies. She can coach you, though."

Grady had seen the story in the papers about Emily Diaz Madison and her past. But apparently she was going to practice as a midwife again. And if the "Tessa" Madison had mentioned was Tessa Rossi, Grady knew the pediatrician and her new husband, Vince. When Tessa was a little girl, Grady and his dad had delivered her first saddle to her. And Vince— He had worked at the saddle shop while Grady was in college.

Madison extended his hand to Grady once more. Grady shook it; then the doctor exited the room.

Immediately, Francesca began, "Grady, I don't know if it's such a good idea for me to stay with you."

"Why not?"

She reflectively glanced down at her stomach, and he did, too. Their gazes met.

He felt a zing to his midsection.

Damn, if there wasn't still chemistry between them. He'd let Francesca cut off personal contact after she'd told him she was pregnant and he'd stipulated she e-mail him with a doctor's report after each visit. He'd had the sense she'd run if he demanded more. He'd also realized the two of them were very different. However, every time one of her reports arrived in his e-mail, he could picture her sleek, long, brown hair lying across his sofa, her body under his, and the way his desire had gotten out of control. In spite of that, he'd kept his distance.

He *wouldn't* let a career woman make a fool of him again. He wouldn't let someone whose values didn't match his play a significant role in his life.

But Francesca Talbot was carrying his child. His son. That meant he had to watch over her. That meant they would be connected for a very long time—if *he* had anything to say about it.

From their first meeting, Grady had guessed Francesca was an independent woman. Having someone take care of her was a hard pill to swallow. He had to tread carefully now or he suspected she'd stubbornly walk the other way.

"We have to put the baby first, don't you think?" he asked.

She worried her lower lip, and he suddenly had the urge to take her into his arms and kiss it.

After studying him for a few long moments, she replied, "If I consider staying with you, I don't want you to hover."

Independent was right. "You have a cell phone. I have a cell phone. I can spend most of my time in the barn. But at least I can get to you within minutes if you need help. Speed dial is a great technological advance."

A small smile crossed her lips at his wry tone. "Do you cook?"

He shrugged. "*Cook* is a relative term, but I told you I come from a big family. My mother or sister drops off meals once or twice a week. I do know a saucepan from a frying pan, though. Most men these days do."

He saw remnants of emotion in her eyes. Memories of men who didn't?

He kept his voice gentle as he would with a spooked mustang. "I know this isn't something you want to do, Francesca. I get it. So why don't you just try it for a couple of days and see what happens? I promise not to wait on you hand and foot. But I'll be close by if you need something."

She sank down onto the hospital bed and he was by her side in an instant. "Are you okay?"

"I'm just tired." When she looked up at him with those big green eyes that packed so much punch, he almost wished he hadn't issued the invitation.

She said simply, "I don't depend on anyone, Grady. That's not me. I wanted to see this pregnancy to its finish on my own."

"I know you did. But this is *my* child, too."

"That's why I called you."

"I'm glad you did."

She stood again, but when she picked up the pharmacy bag on the bed and stuffed it into a larger one on the bedside table, he noticed her hand trembled. Still, as she moved the rest of her toiletries into the bag one-handed, he didn't offer to help.

She explained, "One of the nurses brought me supplies since I didn't know how long I'd be here when this first happened."

"We'll need to stop at your place and pack a suitcase," he suggested.

She raised her gaze to his, and he saw doubts once more.

Stepping toward her, he took her hand from the bag and held it. Her hand was cold. "This is going to be simple, Frannie." He had called her that once before and it had seemed so right. "You're going to stay in my guest bedroom, and I'll be a holler away. That's all there is to it."

"I don't trust easily."

He searched her eyes to find out why, giving her the opportunity to tell him. But she didn't.

"You can lock the door on your bedroom," he kidded. When a guarded look came over her, he added, "I have a great border collie who'll be your watchdog. Will that make you feel better?"

"You really have a dog?"

"His name is Shadow."

"Shadow?"

"I found him alongside the road. A car had hit him. After I took him to the vet and brought him home, he never left my side."

"Tessa didn't tell me about Shadow," she murmured.

"But she told you other things?" Grady arched a brow.

"Not much." Color came into her cheeks because her comment had told him she had asked.

He wasn't going to let this go. "Not much, such as…"

"She told me her dad bought saddles from your father, that you're close to your family and spend a lot of time with them."

"*I* told you that."

"I know, but it made me feel easier that she…confirmed it."

So it was true Francesca didn't trust easily. Not even herself. Why was that?

Did he *need* to know? Did he want to get personally involved with the mother of his baby? It was a ridiculous question, but they certainly could stay removed from each other just like divorced parents did. They were going to have to figure out how they wanted to play this. He had to figure out how *he* was going to play this.

The aide came into the room with the discharge paperwork and Grady was glad for the interruption.

He had a feeling he was going to be spending a lot of time in the barn.

Grady pulled into the driveway that led to a detached two-car garage beside the old Victorian where Francesca lived. He spotted a jewel-toned light shining in the foyer. "Is that on a timer?"

"It is. I set it up after Tessa and Emily moved out."

"How long have you known Tessa?"

"Since Family Tree opened. We consulted on a case and became friends." The Family Tree Health Center in

Lubbock—which offered the best health care in West Texas—housed many professional offices including Tessa's and Francesca's. But the two-story Victorian they'd shared was located in the small town of Sagebrush about fifteen minutes from Lubbock.

Suddenly Grady wished he knew a lot more about Francesca than he did. "How long did Emily live with you?"

"About nine months."

Vince had told him the three women were as tight as sisters. He knew about sisters. His tried to poke into his life when he let her.

Grady opened the door to his truck and came around to Francesca's side. After he opened her door, he extended his hand. She accepted his help until her feet were firmly planted on the ground.

"Are you going to live here by yourself?"

"I'm not sure."

They strolled up the walk, Grady slowing his pace to hers. The early December wind blew and he noticed she shivered.

"You need a heavier jacket," he said gruffly. The light wool jacket she wore wasn't insulated enough for the colder weather.

She turned toward him, her gaze locking to his. "I know that. But when I left this morning, I didn't realize a cold front was moving in."

In the sudden silence he realized he had to back off a little and corral his protective instincts. "Point taken."

After they reached the door, Francesca used her key to unlock it. They stepped inside and the Tiffany light illuminated the foyer.

Grady immediately focused on the steps. "I suppose your bedroom's upstairs?"

"I can handle a flight of stairs," she said absently, as if the thought of them fatigued her more. She might even still fear a miscarriage.

"I know you can. But Madison told you to rest. Tell me what you need and I'll go up and get it." He didn't want her getting dizzy again or feeling weak and falling.

She smiled. "It's not that simple. My suitcase is in the closet. I've got sweaters in one drawer, jeans in another—"

"You have your cell phone, don't you?"

"I do."

"Good. And I have mine. I'll program my number in. You sit on the sofa and call me. You can tell me exactly where everything is you want me to bring down. This doesn't have to be a big deal, Frannie."

She hesitated, then said, "I've never had a nickname."

They were standing close in the small foyer, the heat of the house chasing away the cold. Or was his proximity to Francesca chasing it away? This was the woman who'd set him on fire with a desire he hadn't experienced in years!

Studying her now, he saw she was still pale and the smudges under her eyes were becoming even bluer. She'd had a long, exhausting, traumatic day and he just wanted to get her back to his ranch.

He cleared his throat. "So how about the phone?"

Making up her mind, she slipped her phone from her coat pocket and handed it to him.

"I'll be done in ten minutes tops. Then you can sit in

my favorite recliner with Shadow at your side and I'll bring you whatever you want."

"I'm going to need lots of vegetables," she murmured.

"No problem. I've got a freezer full. They'll only take a few minutes to steam. How does that sound?"

"That sounds great."

He programmed his number into her phone, then handed it back to her. Taking his from his pocket, he jogged up the stairs and at the top called down, "Ring me."

She did. For the next few minutes, their system worked pretty well. Until...

"In the second drawer in the chest I have some—" Francesca hesitated "—some underwear. Just grab a few of the blue and pink ones."

He couldn't help but tease. "Should I ask what the other ones are?"

"They're my nonpregnancy underwear."

He laughed. "It's okay, Frannie. I promise I won't look at them. I'm just packing a few into the suitcase, stuffing them under a sweater." For the most part, he *didn't* look. He knew he had to gather everything quickly or she might change her mind.

Grady was on his way back downstairs when the front door opened and two women spilled in. Tessa Rossi he recognized right away. He supposed the other woman was Emily Madison. They both took one look at him and stopped short. Then they aimed their gazes at Francesca, who was sitting on the sofa in the living room.

Rushing toward her, they gave her hugs.

After a few moments, Tessa released her. Her friend's gaze assessed Grady and the suitcase he was carrying.

"When Francesca called to tell me she was being discharged, she said she's going to your ranch with you."

"Her doctor doesn't think she should be alone." Grady felt defensive, not exactly sure why.

Emily assured Francesca, "On the way here, Tessa and I talked about taking turns staying with you."

"You both have kids to take care of. I'm not going to steal you away from them. Grady insists I won't be any trouble, so I thought I'd try it at least overnight. We'll see how it goes."

Grady saw the way the women exchanged looks. He figured Tessa and Emily knew what had happened between him and Francesca, down to the failed birth control. That made him uncomfortable.

As if sensing that, Tessa left her friend, crossed over to Grady and extended her hand. "Do you remember me?"

"I remember exactly how your eyes lit up when you saw your first saddle."

She smiled. "Vince mentioned you're going to take one of the mustangs he brought back from the sale."

"I sure am. Vince may be able to bring one over this week. I'm looking forward to it."

"She's going to take time," Tessa reminded him. "These horses are used to being in the wild and are not at all happy at being penned up."

"I have a stall ready and the pen outside, too. It'll be okay, Tessa. I'll take good care of her."

Emily had wandered over and now Tessa introduced her. "Grady Fitzgerald, this is Emily Madison."

"You're Dr. Jared Madison's wife?"

Emily nodded and shook his hand, her black, very

curly hair bobbing around her face as she did so. "Yes, I am, though I'm still getting used to the name. We married about six weeks ago."

Grady turned his focus back on Tessa. "And you and Vince married in August?"

"Yes, we did."

Francesca levered herself up, using the arm on the chair. They all could see she looked exhausted.

Emily went to her and gave her another hug. "If there's anything you need, anything at all, you call."

When Emily was finished, Tessa moved toward Francesca and dropped her arm around her. "You know we both mean it."

Francesca nodded. "I know. Thanks for...being here."

Tessa dismissed the thanks with a wave. Her blond hair falling over her shoulder, she followed Emily to the foyer and out the door. They called, "Good night" as they left.

Minutes later, Grady heard a car back out of the driveway. "They really care about you."

"Yes, they do. They're my family now."

"You don't have any family in Sagebrush?"

"I don't have any family at all."

When she said it, he heard pain in her voice. Was that from losing them? Or some deeper reason?

"Come on. Let's get you to my place. After you have something to eat, you can try out my guest bed and sleep as long as you want." He knew she'd made arrangements while at the hospital with the other doctors in her practice to cover for her.

"I can't remember the last time I slept without setting the alarm."

"Tonight, you don't have to set an alarm. You can sleep as late as you want."

When she looked up at him, he saw gratitude in her eyes. And he almost…he almost kissed her. But he knew better than to tangle up their lives any more right now.

He knew better than to become involved with a woman who backed away from emotional intimacy. He'd been deceived and betrayed by a woman who didn't know the meaning of love. He wouldn't risk his heart again.

Chapter Two

Francesca rubbed her damp palms on her pant legs and worked to slow her pulse rate, telling herself to *calm down*.

Grady slanted a glance her way as he drove. "What's wrong?"

"I…I don't think I should have come."

"Are you going to chicken out on me?"

"I'm not chickening out!" Her tone was louder than she intended and she felt her shoulders square.

"That's better. That's the Francesca Talbot I met the first night. You're not any different than you were then. *I'm* not any different than I was then. We obviously got along, so let's just see if we can't get through at least one night."

At that, he pulled into the driveway of a stone and clapboard ranch house and parked. She hurriedly unfas-

tened her seat belt, opened the door and slid out before
he could try to help her. But it was a long way down.
He was there as she landed unsteadily, his hands at her
sides, holding her. "Are you okay?"

"I'm fine. It's just been a while since I maneuvered
in and out of a truck."

"Or off of a horse?" he asked with teasing lights in
his eyes. They sparkled silver under the floodlight that
lit up the front of the house.

"I've never ridden a horse. I've only been around
Vince's lately."

He let out a low whistle. "Well, after this baby's
born, you're going to have to learn. Our son will be
riding a horse by the time he's three."

"Three? Are you out of your mind?"

"With supervision, of course. But let's get you inside."

She wasn't sure if he was trying to rile her on purpose
or tease her. The night they'd met, she'd liked his sense
of humor. Why didn't she appreciate it now?

As Grady unlocked the door, a big black-and-white
dog shot through the opening before Grady could open
the door the whole way. The canine rounded Grady's
legs three times, then sat down in front of him.

Grady leaned down to pet him. "Hi, boy. I brought
someone to meet you. I'd like you to spend a little time
with her so she feels at home here."

Shadow cocked his head at her. She'd like to be
friendly with Grady's dog. She loved animals almost as
much as children.

Slowly she extended her hand. Shadow came forward
cautiously and sniffed her fingers.

She didn't make a move to pet him, waiting to see what he'd do next.

Shadow went through the same antics he had with Grady. "Can I pet you now?" she asked as he finally sat blinking up at her, feeling herself relax a little. She leaned down and gently touched his head. He rolled his head to the side as if he wanted more.

"I think he likes you," Grady decided with a chuckle, and pushed open the door the whole way. He switched on a few lights. "I'll go get your suitcase."

Francesca stood in the entryway, thinking the place didn't look at all like a bachelor pad. There were curtains at the windows in the living room—a burgundy-and-navy plaid—the same material as the sofa. There were two navy, corduroy recliners by the native stone fireplace, braided rugs in tan and navy and wood side cabinets and shelves that housed a collection of hand-painted horses. Framed photographs lined the length of his entertainment center.

When she glanced to her right into the kitchen, she spotted clean, off-white counters, maple cupboards and an oval table big enough to seat six.

"Don't look so surprised," he said with an amused expression as he came in with her suitcase. "What did you expect? A sink filled with dishes? Coffee rings on all the tables? Newspapers scattered about?"

"I didn't know what to expect. I don't know you, Grady, and I'm still not sure I should be here."

He looked at her curiously. "I never thought you'd be this jumpy about it. We slept together. How much more personal can that get? Spending the night here shouldn't be a big deal."

Grady might be perceptive sometimes, but he didn't know her. He didn't realize how hard it was for her to trust. That she still bore the effects of a past that she was trying to shake off and didn't know if she ever could. Her turmoil must have shown in her eyes.

Approaching her slowly, he rested his hand on her shoulder. She was supposed to feel comfort. But there was more…a zingy pull toward him that had affected her since the night they'd met. She backed away, unconsciously trying to create enough distance so she could think.

But he clearly took it for something else. "You've had a difficult day. More than difficult. I'm surprised you're still on your feet. Come on, let me show you to your bedroom. If you do want to leave tomorrow, we'll think of another plan."

We'll think of another plan.

She absolutely wasn't used to teaming up. Sure, Emily and Tessa were around for support. But she made up her own mind and made her own decisions. She'd done that since the night she'd had to defend her mother from her father—one very big decision that had changed all of their lives.

Reflexively, she touched her left ear. She'd lost some hearing in that ear because of that night. But only Emily, Tessa and Vince knew that. Somehow she manufactured a smile. "I promise I won't look for scattered newspapers or coffee rings along the way."

He didn't return her smile, just looked troubled. Maybe he was realizing having a stranger in his house wouldn't be easy. They really *were* strangers, no matter how intimate they'd been.

His gaze locked to hers, and she felt an elemental tug toward him. But he turned and headed down the hall. She followed him into the guest bedroom.

Grady settled the suitcase on the black metal-and-wood bed. "That door leads to your bathroom. You can reach it from the hall, too. I've got one in the master suite so you don't have to worry about being interrupted. And all of the doors *do* lock."

In some ways she felt foolish about her reluctance to stay, in others she just felt totally off-balance. She took off her jacket and laid it on the patchwork quilt next to the suitcase. "Thank you for offering me a place to stay tonight so that I'd have someone close by."

His penetrating blue eyes searched for the truth in hers. "I want you to get some rest. I want our baby to have the best chance at life."

He was only doing this because of his son. She'd better not weave anything else into it. "I've been talking to this baby ever since I learned I was pregnant. But now that I know he's a boy, our conversation might change a little."

Grady smiled. "You're going to discuss football with him?"

"I don't know. I'll have to think about it." She laughed.

A few feet separated them, yet at that moment, Francesca felt closer to Grady than she had all evening.

The doorbell rang.

Grady groaned. "I told her not to come over tonight."

"Who?" Francesca asked.

"My mother. I phoned her about the accident."

"You told her I'd be staying here?" Francesca couldn't keep her voice from rising.

"You're already pregnant. It's not as if anything else is going to happen," he offered wryly as he left the room and went to answer the door.

Francesca wasn't sure what to do—hide and unpack her suitcase or go and face Grady's mother. She was exhausted. But this woman would be her child's grandmother. Didn't she want her baby to have a loving family in his life?

Loving. Maybe Grady's mother wouldn't even like her. Maybe Grady's mother was going to disapprove of this whole situation.

Francesca couldn't help but go to the mirror over the dresser and take a peek at herself. She wished she hadn't. She looked as if she'd been in an accident. If only she could just drop into bed. And yet she couldn't. She had to check her sugar with the meter and supplies the pharmacy had sent up before she left the hospital and make sure she ate something—the *right* food.

Life had gotten way too complicated today, and she knew that wasn't going to change any time soon.

As Francesca walked down the hall to the kitchen, she smelled cooked food. She wasn't sure what kind, but her stomach grumbled.

An attractive woman who might have been in her sixties, with reddish-brown, chin-length hair laced with gray and rimless glasses turned her way.

"Aren't you going to introduce us, Grady?" mother asked son.

This was an awkward situation in so many ways, but Francesca shored up any energy she still possessed and walked right into it.

"Mom, this is Francesca Talbot. Francesca, this is my mother, Maureen Fitzgerald. When I told her I was going to bring you here, she decided to load up the refrigerator."

Maureen gave her son a jab in the ribs. "Don't be ridiculous. I know you can cook. But I also know you're busy. And having a guest—" She stopped. "Well, I just thought you both might like something homemade." She studied Francesca. "Did you have supper?"

"There was a tray in the hospital around five, but I wasn't very hungry."

"No, I guess not. Not after the day you've had. Grady told me you have a sugar problem, so I grilled lean ground beef patties and cooked brown rice. There's a tossed salad and broccoli with cheese that's still warm. We can zap it in the microwave if you need it hotter."

His mother searched his cabinet for serving dishes.

"Mom, please."

Maureen stared at him. "What?"

"I asked you to wait until tomorrow to come over, didn't I?"

"Yes, you did. But I thought you'd need supper tonight, and obviously you do."

Grady looked exasperated. "Francesca needs to get her feet up and turn in. She's not going to want to eat a heavy meal."

Shadow had come along with Francesca and now sat beside her at the table, glancing between Grady and his mother.

Francesca was afraid Grady had hurt his mother's feelings. "Actually, Grady, maybe I could just have half of one of those patties and a few stalks of broccoli. Everything smells delicious. I'll wait for a while after I eat before I turn in."

"You won't be able to keep your eyes open."

She gave him a look and Maureen saw it. His mother also seemed to notice the way Shadow stayed by Francesca's side.

Before Grady could protest further, Maureen took a dish from the cupboard and a serving spoon from the drawer. Then she cut and slid half of a patty and a serving of broccoli onto a dish. She set it on the table.

"Did *you* eat?" she asked her son.

"Yes, I did."

"Good." Maureen snagged a glass from the cupboard and a jug of milk from the refrigerator. Pouring it half-full, she handed it to Francesca. "So…Grady tells me you're a neonatologist."

"Thank you. Yes, I am. With this arm it's going to be hard to doctor for the next month. But I'll figure out a way."

"Maybe you could take some time off," Maureen suggested.

"I'm going to take a few days, but then I really need to work. There are several preemie babies and we're going to be short-staffed. One of the doctors in my practice is going out of town."

Although her mind was sluggish due to her fatigue, Francesca made a stab at continuing the conversation. "Grady told me he has an older brother, a younger brother and a younger sister. Do they all live in this area?"

"Yes, they do, and I'm so glad of that. It gives us all a chance to get together often. Liam lived in Amarillo for a while when he was married, but since his divorce he's back in Sagebrush. Do you have family here?" Maureen asked as Grady leaned against the counter and crossed his arms over his chest.

"No, I don't." Francesca didn't say more.

"Do they live somewhere else in the state?" Maureen pressed.

"No, actually I don't have family. My mother died a few years ago before I moved here. We lived in Oklahoma then."

"And your father?"

Suddenly Francesca wasn't hungry at all. She didn't travel this route often. "My parents were separated when I was a child."

"And you didn't continue to see your father?"

Francesca made it as simple as she could. "No. We moved away, my mother and I."

"But he was still—"

Grady cut in. "Mom, maybe we'd better cut this short."

Maureen examined the two of them, then agreed. "I guess we should. I was simply concerned this might be my only chance to talk to Francesca. You've told us about her, but this is the first glimpse I've had of her. She's carrying my grandchild."

Whatever Grady had told his mother had apparently caused her some consternation. "Mrs. Fitzgerald, if you'd like to talk to me, I can give you my number."

That seemed to surprise Maureen. "You'd do that?"

Francesca's eyebrows arched. What *exactly* had Grady told his mother about her? "Yes, I would."

Maureen seemed to relax a bit. "Well, that would

be nice. Maybe you could join our family for dinner some Sunday."

"Mom," Grady warned, as if they'd had a conversation about this, but she wasn't sticking to the script.

How comfortable or uncomfortable would dinner with the Fitzgerald family be? Francesca felt as if she'd just landed on a foreign planet and was treading her way very carefully. "I'll certainly think about that."

His mother didn't look satisfied, but she didn't look altogether put off, either. She nodded to Francesca. "You go ahead and eat. I'll leave. I would appreciate having your number."

With a grunt Grady said, "I'll give it to her." He scribbled something on a piece of paper and handed it to his mom.

Francesca took a bite of the broccoli and said to Maureen, "This is very good. Thank you for bringing it over tonight."

Grady's mother smiled at her. "You're welcome."

After Grady walked his mother to the door, they stepped outside together and had a few moments of conversation. Francesca couldn't overhear. It was probably just as well.

When Grady came back in, he shook his head. "I'm sorry about all that. She's a strong-willed woman. And my sister is just like her."

Francesca laughed and it felt so good to do it. "She meant well." Francesca took another bite of the broccoli, then asked, "What did you tell her about us? About how this happened?"

Grady ran his fingers through his hair. "I didn't say

much. I just told my family that you were pregnant and that we were giving each other some space until the baby was born."

"They thought we were involved?"

"I was vague."

If she had family who cared about her, would she have told them that she'd had a one-night stand? She didn't know why she was even wondering. Having family had only ever hurt her.

"Does your family interfere in your life often?"

Shadow bumped her leg, as if he wanted to share her supper, or the remains of it. But she didn't know if she should feed him.

The question she'd just asked Grady apparently caused him some annoyance because he was scowling at her. "What's that supposed to mean?"

"You said you asked your mother not to come tonight, but she came anyway. Don't you consider that interference?"

"Would you have considered it interference if your mother had stopped by?"

She wasn't touching that question with the proverbial ten-foot pole. "I thought only lawyers answered questions with questions."

Digging his thumbs into his hip pockets, he paused for a moment, then responded, "My mother likes to look after her family. It's as simple as that. She does what she thinks best. I don't always agree with her and I tell her that."

After Francesca finished her milk, she set down her glass. "It *was* very kind of her to bring over dinner."

That seemed to take the wind out of Grady's annoyed sails. He glanced at her empty plate. "I think you really *did* like it."

She motioned to the food on the counter. "Do you want help stowing that away?"

"No, I'll take care of it. You put your feet up. That's what you're supposed to do."

"I'm going to take a shower first. Do you have something I can wrap around my cast?"

After rummaging in a bottom cupboard, he pulled something out of a box. "Here's a plastic bag. Do you need help taping it on?"

She shook her head. "I'll be fine. I have to take off my clothes first."

That brought a look into his blue eyes that she'd seen the night they'd had sex. It was an intense look that told her maybe he was imagining that night all over again.

Before that movie could play in *her* head, she had to make her getaway. She said, "I'll see you in the morning."

Without waiting for a good-night, she hurried down the hall. She didn't know why she was so skittish around him. Sure, he'd seen her naked. Sure, they'd talked a few hours, sexual tension bumping back and forth between them. The problem was, she still got butterflies when she looked into his eyes. And that would never do. She didn't want a relationship with Grady. She didn't want a relationship with anyone…except her baby. And Tessa and Emily, she added as an afterthought.

Francesca decided to wait to test her blood sugar until after she was out of the shower. But she was suddenly more tired than she'd been before. Maybe it was the warm food in her stomach. Maybe the day had finally just taken her to the end of her rope. The cast on her arm made everything more difficult, especially dressing and undressing. It took her much longer than she planned, and when she was finished she almost felt like crying. That was ridiculous. She didn't cry.

Hormones?

Sure.

Attaching the plastic bag around her cast wasn't easy, either. Stepping into the shower, using one hand to turn on the water, bathe and soap her hair took more energy and ingenuity than she thought she had. Finally, when she was finished, she stepped out of the bathtub, toweled off and realized she hadn't packed a nightgown. She hadn't really packed. Grady had. She'd simply forgotten about the nightwear.

Wrapping a towel around herself, she tucked it in the best she could, then searched through her suitcase to find something to wear to bed. Panties and a bra she couldn't hook? A sweater?

Finally she sank down onto the bed and dropped her head into her hand, her wet hair falling along her cheeks.

She heard scratching at her door. A knock followed.

She groaned. She was not up to more conversation.

"Francesca, Shadow wants to come in to say goodnight. Do you mind?"

"I'm not dressed," she called.

"He won't mind."

She actually almost laughed. "Will you be coming in with him?"

"Only if you want me to."

"Let Shadow in. Maybe he can help me find something to wear to bed. I forgot to list a nightgown in the items you were picking up."

There was silence. Then the door opened and the border collie barged in. He didn't even hesitate, but jumped up on the bed and licked her face. She put her arm around him and felt real tears burn in her eyes.

Seconds later she felt a male presence. Lifting her head, she saw Grady towering over her. "Am I going to have privacy staying here with you?" Her voice trembled a bit and she hated that.

"You'll have your privacy. But right now I think you need this more." He handed her a white, button-down silk shirt.

"This looks like a good dress shirt."

"I don't have any weddings or funerals in the near future, so wear it. Do you want Shadow in or out?"

"In is fine." She didn't want to admit to Grady that his dog seemed to understand her. How odd was that?

"Do you need help getting that bag off your arm?"

She had taped it the best she could, probably with more tape than was necessary. Pulling it all off could take a while.

Although she hadn't answered him, he sat down on the bed beside her and started ripping tape from the plastic. It took him no time at all. "I had my arm in a cast once. It's no picnic, especially when it still hurts."

"When I get settled and stop moving around it will be okay."

His fingers edged the top of the cast first. Then he

slid them down and touched her fingertips sticking out from the bottom of the cast. "You're cold," he said.

"I just got out of the shower."

"Did you say you had to test your blood sugar?"

"Yes."

"Do you want me to be here when you do?"

She looked over at him. "You want to be part of that, too?"

"Your health is important to the life of our baby. I should know what's going on."

She sighed. "Give me five minutes to get into your shirt."

Grady returned five minutes later. She'd dropped her towel, donned his shirt and finally managed to roll the cuff above her cast. At least she was buttoned from neck to thigh. The material of the shirt wasn't much different from a nightgown, and it molded to her when she stood.

After reading the meter instructions, she'd laid out everything she needed on the bed and prepared the lancet.

Grady pulled the rocker up to her so he could see what she was doing.

They were knee to knee, tantalizingly close.

She moved her leg away so it didn't brush his. She was much too aware that he'd probably shaved before he'd picked her up. His jawline was clean. She was also aware that he'd slapped on cologne, an outdoor scent that reminded her of trees and woods and places she'd never been.

Grady watched intently as she inserted the test strip into the machine, used an alcohol wipe and pricked her finger to collect a drop of blood.

She studied the readout. "High-normal. But it hasn't been two hours since I ate, so that makes sense."

Changing his position on the bed, Shadow crossed one paw over the other and settled his head on his paws. When she stood and crossed the room to set the meter on the dresser, she looked in the mirror and saw Grady watching her.

"What?" she asked, knowing the bulge of her tummy was evident under the soft shirt.

"You look better in that shirt than *I* ever did."

"Are you trying to flatter me?"

Now he didn't keep his distance. He walked right up to her and stood very close. "You're a beautiful woman, Francesca. I don't know many men who could see you like that and not want to look."

"You looked before," she murmured, knowing her cheeks were flaming.

"That was different."

"Different, how?"

"You weren't carrying my child then. Now it makes a difference." He lifted a wet strand of hair away from her face. "You didn't have wet hair then, either."

"I don't have the energy to dry it."

"Let me do it for you."

"Oh, Grady…" she whispered.

"I brought you here to help you. What good is help if you won't accept it?"

Emily and Tessa told her all the time that she didn't know how to accept help, that she took on too much all by herself and felt she had to do it all. She was so sleepy right now, she wouldn't mind falling asleep with wet hair.

But Grady was insistent. "Do you have a brush?"

She gestured toward the bag on her bed, knowing the one the nurse had bought for her at the pharmacy was somewhere inside.

After Grady moved the cane-backed rocker over to an outlet, he motioned for her to sit in the chair and plugged in the hair dryer that he'd brought from the bathroom. She hadn't remembered *that,* either.

"Grady, you really don't have to—"

He switched on the hair dryer, ignoring her protest. She expected just a quick ruffle and brush through and they'd soon be finished. Damp hair didn't matter to her. But that wasn't the way Grady did it. He was careful, oh so careful. In fact, he wasn't simply careful. Each brush-stroke felt seductive. He took his time, brushing her hair away from her face, making sure the air didn't hit her eyes or her mouth or her nose. With each stroke she sank deeper into relaxation. With each stroke, she remembered the touch of his callused fingers on her skin—

When he switched off the dryer, she looked up at him. "I don't think I can move a muscle."

"You don't have far to go, though I think Shadow's going to take up half your bed. Are you sure you want him here?"

"I'd like him to stay." It was on the tip of her tongue to say, "I'd like *you* to stay." That was absolutely insane. She was only here because she needed a little bit of help.

The idea of a bond or an involvement or a relationship with Grady Fitzgerald terrified her. When she was small she had often hidden in a closet to be safe from her father. The day she'd found courage to protect her mother from him, he'd hit her, drawn blood and caused her hearing loss. For the most part she'd worked through her childhood over the years. Two years ago, when she'd decided her fear of relationships was foolhardy, she'd chosen the wrong man.

No, she wasn't ready to take even a few slow steps into a relationship. Her focus now was her baby. Nothing else.

Rousing herself from the fatigue and exhaustion that had finally caught up with her, she stood and moved to the bed—away from Grady's hands…away from his strength…away from anything that would tempt her heart.

Shadow gazed up at her when she slipped under the covers.

Grady laid the hair dryer on the dresser. "If you need anything, I'm across the hall."

She nodded. But she knew she wouldn't. Not from him.

Grady exited the room and closed the door behind him. She turned on her side, placing her hand on Shadow's warm coat, totally aware of Grady's shirt against her skin.

Chapter Three

When Francesca awoke the following morning, she was disoriented for a few seconds. Then she realized where she was—at Grady's ranch.

She patted Shadow on the head and he barked. Shortly after, there was a rap on the door. "Francesca— are you up?"

Hearing his master's voice, Shadow jumped off the bed. Making sure she was covered by the sheet, as well as buttoned to the neck in Grady's shirt, she called, "Not quite. But you can come in."

Grady opened the door and stepped inside. He was wearing a many-times-washed T-shirt today, jeans and the ever-present boots. She didn't think any man had ever looked sexier. Quickly she pushed that thought away as Shadow trotted into the hall.

"Do you need anything?" he asked. "Tessa's dad and Vince are bringing the mustang over, so I'll be heading to the barn as soon as I grab a cup of coffee."

"I'm going to scramble myself an egg," she said, knowing she must look a mess. "I could make more than one if you're interested."

His blue eyes were more than interested as they locked with hers and she felt a little tremor ripple through her. How could she be attracted to him when her life was a mess right now?

"I'll scramble the eggs," he offered, "as soon as I let Shadow out. You're supposed to be resting. Remember? That's why you're here."

Granted, that was the reason for her being here, but she couldn't let him do too much for her. She couldn't become dependent on him. She'd taken care of herself all of her life, and she wasn't going to stop now.

Instead of keeping a bit of distance between them, he ambled into the room and loomed over her.

Her chin came up and she straightened her shoulders.

A puzzled expression crossed his face as he lowered himself to the bed, right beside her hip. "You haven't told me yet why I spook you."

"You don't," she protested quickly, as if that would answer his question.

He shook his head. "You've changed since the night we met."

Sure she had. That night, he'd been an attractive man she'd met in the crowd. That night, she hadn't been pregnant with his child. That night, she hadn't been scared to death of feelings for him that had taken root a little deeper each time they'd talked. That night, for once in her life, she'd simply let go.

Look where that had gotten her!

"You've changed, too," she answered, knowing she had to go on the offensive. "You weren't protective and hovering. You weren't trying to tell me what was best for my baby."

"Do you think that's what I'm doing now?" he asked without getting angry, and that surprised her.

"I don't know, Grady."

"If you were staying with Tessa, would you mind if she made you breakfast?"

She thought about that and easily knew the answer. "No, I suppose not."

"At least you're honest." His tone was wry.

"I try to be."

He nodded to her arm. "How does it feel?"

"It aches a little, but nothing I can't handle."

He rose to his feet. "There isn't much you can't handle, is there?"

"Do you want me to answer that, or was it a rhetorical question?"

"It was rhetorical. I'll make those eggs and then get out of your hair for a while. Maybe you'll relax if I'm in the barn."

As Francesca watched him leave, she breathed a sigh of relief. Maybe she *could* relax if he was in the barn. But she doubted it. Because she was still carrying his child.

Francesca saw the horse trailer roll in. She heard men's voices and recognized Vince's and Walter McGuire's.

She'd only met Tessa's dad a few times, but she knew his history with Vince. When Vince fell in love with Tessa in high school, Mr. McGuire had disapproved. After Tessa had gotten pregnant and decided to marry Vince, her father had disowned her. Later in her pregnancy, she'd lost her baby and almost died. She and Vince had gone their separate ways until this past spring when he'd returned to town with his best friend's baby and they'd fallen in love all over again. He and Tessa were married now, and as happy as could be, raising Vince's little boy as well as adopting a little girl. Besides that, Vince and Tessa's dad seemed to have found some common ground and were putting the past aside.

It was hard for Francesca to remain still and rest as her doctor had suggested. But she'd do anything for this baby. So she sat on the sofa, making notes for anyone who covered for her at the hospital this week.

When the door opened, she expected to see Grady. Instead, her gaze landed on Tessa's husband.

Vince grinned at her as he came in the door. "Hey there, I told Tessa I'd stop in and see how you were doing. I think she and Emily are planning to come over tomorrow."

She could use her best friends' company, but was glad to see Vince, too. Since she'd gotten to know him over the summer, he was almost like a big brother.

"I'm glad you stopped in. I'm supposed to rest and…" She grimaced. "I'm not used to doing that."

Vince sat on a chair across from the sofa and petted Shadow. "Hi there, boy. Are you keeping Francesca company?"

The dog cocked his head, gave a little bark in answer and then settled his head on his paws again.

"I can imagine resting for the sake of resting is a headache," Vince said.

"So you brought over a mustang?"

"Yep. Grady wanted one. It's quite an adjustment for those horses, captured from the wild, being hauled off to auction. But they make wonderful companion horses once they're gentled. They're good workers, too."

"How many horses does Grady have?"

"You haven't been to the barn?"

"I've never been here before, Vince."

His face darkened a little. "I'm sorry. Tessa keeps her friends' lives private. I thought maybe you'd spent some time here."

"No. After I found out I was pregnant, I thought it was better if Grady and I kept our distance. It would help us both to figure things out."

Vince's brows arched. "When two people share a child, they've got to tell each other what's going on in their heads."

"You know why I might be reluctant to do that."

Tessa had known Francesca's background soon after they'd moved in together. But one night this summer, when Francesca had visited the couple, she'd felt comfortable enough with Vince to fill him in.

His eyes were gentle as he said, "I know you've had a rough time with men. My father was an alcoholic—thank God, not a violent one—so I understand a little bit of what you went through. And that doctor you got involved with, I know he was more of the same."

"Darren isn't an alcoholic."

"No, but abuse is abuse."

Francesca remembered her relationship with Darren all too well. She remembered the day she'd left him—for all the right reasons.

"I don't know what happened the night I met Grady. I don't know why—" she waved at her tummy "—this happened. It was so out of character for me."

"Maybe you were just tired of guarding yourself so well. Maybe you sensed Grady was a different kind of man."

"Is he?" She sought her answer in Vince's eyes.

"When I worked at his dad's saddle shop, he was around now and then during school breaks. I've got to admit, I was jealous of his relationship with his dad. They worked together like a father and son *should*. They talked. They joked. They seemed to enjoy each other's company. Grady was older than I was, but he never ordered me around. He taught me what needed to be done and he was patient."

She thought about what Vince had said. "He and I are very different, Vince. Not only our backgrounds, but who we are. You know how much time I spend at the hospital. You know those babies mean everything to me."

"But now *your* baby is going to mean the world to you."

"Yes, he is. I'll figure out a way to work and take care of him. I don't know if I want to share those responsibilities. I already love him more than I've ever loved anyone, so when I think about handing over my baby to someone else, even for a couple of hours—

What if Grady demands joint custody? What if he wants equal time?"

"Whoa! You're getting ahead of yourself. Do you want some advice?"

Vince was a good guy and he wouldn't steer her wrong. "Sure."

"Watch what Grady does, rather than thinking about what he doesn't say."

Advice was one thing, a riddle was another. "Am I supposed to know what that means?"

"I think you'll figure it out. The important thing is you can understand the measure of a man by his actions. Watch Grady—with you, with the horses, with Shadow here, with Tessa and Emily if they come to visit. Watch him until this baby is born, and then decide whether or not he's going to make a good father."

"That makes sense."

"Good." He reached out and patted Shadow's head again. "I'll tell Tessa you're already on the mend." He rose to his feet.

"Thanks, Vince."

He reached down and squeezed her shoulder. "No thanks necessary. We're friends. Friends look out for each other."

Grady entered his house, not knowing where he'd find Francesca. She was supposed to be resting, but she had a mind of her own. He had to wonder just how much she wanted this baby. After all, an unexpected pregnancy could mess up a career woman's life. His resentment of Susan's actions still caused a bitter taste in his mouth.

He was surprised to find Francesca asleep on the sofa, curled on her side, Shadow on the floor close at hand. When he saw his master, he came running over to him.

Grady hunched down, scratched the dog behind the ears and said softly, "So you've been watching over her? Does she give *you* a hard time, too?"

Grady had checked his cell phone about every fifteen minutes to see if he'd missed her call, if she'd left a message because she needed something. But she hadn't. He noticed the list on the coffee table, the medical terms in her pretty handwriting.

Her long, dark hair glimmered with red highlights in the afternoon sun streaming through the window. She was so beautiful. He almost felt as if he were awakening a princess.

He crouched down beside her. "Frannie."

Her eyes opened and she stared up at him in bemusement for a moment. Then reality hit. She hiked herself up and rubbed her face with her hand. "Grady. I must have dozed off. What time is it?"

"Almost one. Did you have lunch?"

"No. I was thinking about getting up and decided to close my eyes for just a little while. I guess I fell asleep. Did Vince leave?"

"A long time ago. I've been doing chores in the barn, getting the new horse settled."

He was making conversation when all he wanted to do was sit down on that sofa and take her into his arms. There was no defiance in her eyes now, or rebelliousness. This was the woman he'd seen the night he met her. This was the woman who had captivated him so. He wondered how long it would be until she brought back the emotional armor.

"What would you like for lunch?" he asked. "We have leftovers from last night. I also stopped at a deli before I picked you up, so I have sandwich fixings, too."

"Leftovers sound good."

Before she became that guarded woman again, he had a question that had been nudging him. Now was as good a time to ask her as any. "What does the baby feel like when he moves?"

Francesca's green gaze locked to his. In that moment a spark of understanding flashed in her eyes—that he had a role in her pregnancy…that he was asking out of more than idle curiosity. He had no idea what she'd say or do.

Unexpectedly, she answered his question with one of her own. "Do you want to feel him when he moves?"

Before he could think better of it, he answered, "Yes."

She closed her eyes for a moment, and then laid her hand on the right side of her tummy atop her sweatshirt. "You can feel him move here."

He told himself he just wanted to feel the baby. There wouldn't be anything intimate about his touch.

But when he laid his hand where hers had been, when he could feel the heat under the material and then the flutter of movement, he knew touching her this way was *very* intimate.

"What was it like the first time *you* felt him move?"

"I was brushing my teeth," she responded with a smile that aroused him even more than touching her had. She went on, "And I felt this little wave, a little rustle, and I realized my baby was moving!"

He didn't correct her by insisting this was his baby, too, because he suddenly realized every woman carrying a child must feel that total union. No man could ever fully understand pregnancy…carrying a life…bringing a miracle into this world.

He didn't move his hand away. He couldn't. He wanted to feel his child's life again. "Have you given any thought to names?"

"I have. A doctor I worked with in Oklahoma—he was my attending and mentored me—was a member of the National Guard, and he was called up and deployed to the Middle East. He was killed there. His name was Joshua. I like the name. But…" she hesitated. "I imagine you have some suggestions, too."

Before her accident, had she decided to share the naming process with him? Could they compromise? He was sensing that they were both strong-willed. What did that mean for the chance of them parenting success-fully together?

One step at a time, he told himself. "I like the name Michael. It was my grandfather's."

He knew he had to stand, move away from her, make them some lunch. But his hand stayed on her stomach. He felt their baby move again. They seemed to lean a little closer to each other.

Then she leaned back and took a breath.

He took the signal for what it was—her defense mech-anisms shifting into place. His had better do the same.

Withdrawing his hand, he stood. "I'm going to wash up, and then I'll get us that lunch."

She lowered her gaze to Shadow, slid her fingers into

the ruff of fur at his neck. "I'm going to call the hospital. I need to check on one of my patients."

"Fine," he replied, and walked away.

He had to walk away for now...until their baby was born. Then he'd be in Francesca's life, whether she wanted him there or not.

Francesca took the last sip of her milk and set down the glass. Conversation had lagged over lunch and she wasn't sure how to pick it up. "How many horses do you have?"

"We're not on a date, Frannie. You don't have to make conversation if you don't feel like it. I'll go back to the barn and you'll have your privacy again."

"No! I mean, this is your house. You should feel comfortable in it. And I'm not just making conversation. I want to know."

He gave her an I-don't-really-believe-that look, but answered her. "I have four horses now—with the mustang."

"What kind are the others?"

His gaze narrowed a bit. "I have a quarter horse, one part Arabian and one part Tennessee walker."

"Have you had them long?"

"There's not a simple answer to that one. Dad always had horses. When I took over the ranch and the business, I kept them."

She absorbed that, not knowing if she should ask any more personal questions.

"What?" he asked.

"You grew up here?"

"Sure did. And I couldn't let mom and dad sell the

ranch when they moved to the retirement community in Lubbock."

"Do they like it there?"

"They do. Mom babysits a lot for my sister, Laurie, and my older brother, John. They've also made friends there who they can socialize with. Dad's on the hospital board and still comes to the shop a few days a week."

"Your mom mentioned a younger brother—Liam?"

"Yes. He moved back to Sagebrush about six months ago. He lives in town."

She remembered the names from the stories he'd related that first night. He'd also told her he spent every Sunday with his family. She could hardly imagine what it was like to sit down with a family, have a peaceful dinner with everybody actually wanting to be together. She and her parents had lived in a vacuum in California. Her father had had his drinking buddies, true, but he had isolated her mother. Her mother had been scared to death to even go to the store without asking her dad first. And after she and her mother had fled to Oklahoma, they'd kept to themselves.

"You mentioned you lost your mom," he prompted.

He was leaving the subject open for her if she wanted to talk about it. She didn't, but she couldn't go completely quiet on the subject or he'd ask more questions later. "My mother died four years ago."

"And that was in Oklahoma."

"Yes."

"So what brought you to Sagebrush?"

This conversation had started because she'd asked

him about his horses. She wished she could go back to that subject.

But since Sagebrush was small, residents could have long memories. She might as well tell him something about Darren. "I met a doctor at a medical conference. We had a long-distance relationship for a while. He was from Lubbock and he asked me to move here."

"So you did."

"Yes, I did. But it didn't work out. I moved in with Tessa, and the rest, as they say, is history. We shared the house together for a year before Emily moved in with us."

"And now you're there alone."

She didn't respond.

Pushing his plate away, he asked casually, "Have you decided what you're going to do about working after the baby's born?"

She became wary. "Not yet."

He leaned forward and placed his hand over hers. She was at once electrified and scared by the feeling. But she didn't pull away...no man's touch had ever made her feel the way Grady's did.

His eyes seemed to become a deeper blue as he assured her, "You don't have to make all the decisions yourself."

"I've made decisions for myself for as long as I can remember."

He leaned back and his jaw set. "I told you before I want to be involved in my son's life."

"I understand that. But all this is very new to me and I'm taking each step carefully. Right now, all I'm concerned about is my baby's health. Surely, you can see that."

The look in his eyes gentled a bit. "I can see it. That's one reason why I think you should stay here through the weekend to make sure your sugar is stable, your arm is healing and you don't overdo it when you shouldn't."

If she stayed, she might find out who Grady really was…what kind of father he might be. She had to know if custody became an issue. "If I'm not in the way, if I don't interfere in your life too much, I'll stay until Sunday."

Somehow she had to figure out how to let Grady help her while maintaining her independence. If *that* wasn't a dilemma!

All she knew right now was that Monday she'd be returning to work.

After all, her career was her baby's future, too.

Dressed in Grady's shirt that night, cold with the early December wind blowing against the house, Francesca went into the bathroom and retrieved her meter from on top of the sink. She wasn't sure whether to hate the little device or be grateful for it. Every time she used it she thought about everything that could go wrong. On the other hand, using it protected her baby's health, as well as her own. After washing her hands, she inserted the test strip into the device, pricked her finger and let the drop of blood flow onto the strip.

"Does that hurt?"

Francesca smelled leather, damp flannel and man. Mixed with all of it was Grady's unique scent. She remembered nuzzling his shoulder—

"I use a different finger each time. It's not bad." The silky shirt had molded to her as she'd prepared materials and used the machine. Now Grady was staring at her tummy under the fabric. His gaze on her was like a caress.

She tried to keep her tone light. "I'm going to have weight to lose after the baby's born."

"Not much. You haven't gained weight anywhere but at your stomach."

Where he'd laid his hand this afternoon. Yes, he could tell where her weight was and wasn't.

She checked the meter readout.

"Good or bad?"

"It's good. Your mom's cooking must be just what I need."

"If I tell her that she'll be here every day, so I'd better do some cooking and see how we do."

Francesca started putting everything away, but he stilled her hand. "I know you're determined to go home Sunday. But will you be able to take good care of yourself? How can you cook with one hand?"

"You'd be surprised what I can do with one hand," she teased.

They both must be remembering the same pictures because she could feel her cheeks heat up and she thought he looked a little flushed, too.

"I promise you, Grady, I'll continue to check my sugar levels. I *will* take care of myself. This baby means everything to me."

"You aren't thinking of asking for sole custody, are you?" He released her and held up his hand. "Before you answer that, you should think about the benefits of having me share care of our baby, and of having an extended family who will love this child, too."

The idea of an extended family panicked her. Would they be judging her? Would they be waiting for her to mess up so Grady could have more control?

"Hey, what did I say?" he asked, looking at her curiously.

"Nothing."

The bathroom was small. Grady was close.

"We have to be honest with each other, Frannie, or we'll never have a good chance to be parents together."

"I can't tell you all my thoughts."

"Just the important ones," he prompted.

What to say and what not to say? "You and I see family very differently. Besides, I have the feeling that yours could all gang up on me to persuade me to see their way—your way."

"I wouldn't let them do that."

She searched his eyes, looking for the truth, hunting for what she'd never found before. The moment was fraught with memories of that night on his couch, the hunger in his kiss, the sensual magic of his touch. She couldn't be seduced by chemistry, or a roughly handsome face or gentle hands that could easily turn not quite so gentle.

He leaned in closer and she would have backed away, but his words were as seductive as everything else about him. "I won't hurt you, Frannie. I won't hurt our baby. And I certainly don't want to get hurt myself. We don't have to jump into anything. We can just take it as it comes."

With that, his lips settled on hers, gently nibbled, then claimed a real kiss. Soon her good hand was on his shoulder, her other at her side. But he wouldn't let her be awkward about it. He slipped his fingers around her waist, pressed her growing child against him and tasted Francesca thoroughly and well.

Francesca felt dizzy. The kind of dizzy that could make her lose her good sense…and her perspective…and her heart. She knew she should run in the other direction. But Grady's hands held her, gently but firmly. His kisses promised passion that she already knew was red-hot. But that one night had been an aberration. She didn't talk to strange men for an evening and then have sex with them. Maybe what she'd been trying to prove to herself that night was that she was still a woman in every sense of the word…that a man other than Darren could desire her.

She hadn't counted on that night affecting her so. She hadn't counted on ever seeing Grady again. But now here she was, pregnant with his child, staying at his ranch. His attitude could turn in a minute and his concern for her could change to a need to control. She had to watch for it. She had to make sure she wasn't sinking into a situation like that again. Not with her baby involved.

For one thing was true. She would never stay with a man like her father. That's why she'd broken off her relationship with Darren. That's why she had to watch Grady carefully.

This was always the awkward part, ending desire too soon.

Even before she'd pulled away, Grady had let go. He didn't turn away to catch his breath. He didn't look down on her as if she were the one with something lacking. Rather, he said, "You really don't want to be here, do you?"

"No," she admitted.

"And you really didn't want me to kiss you."

"That one's not so easy."

He looked surprised her answer wasn't definitive. She was surprised, too.

"Then I didn't read the signals wrong."

"You read confused signals," she responded with a sigh, turning away from him and the sink, thinking about running, yet knowing she had to stay and explain. "I'm attracted to you, Grady. That's obvious." She turned from him.

But he was quick and caught her before she entered her room. "You can run for a while, but eventually you're going to have to tell me what's going on in your head."

"No, I don't have to tell you. That's the point. We have separate lives. We're going to *live* separate lives. The baby might bring us together every now and then, but we probably won't know each other any better then than we do now."

"You're wrong about that." There was an edge to his tone. "I intend to learn everything I possibly can about you. By understanding you, I'll understand our child."

She was startled by his insight and she didn't like it. Yet she knew he was right. "Don't try to close me in, Grady. I'll just work that much harder to break away."

"Is that a threat?"

"No. That's just the way I am."

Shadow had padded into the bathroom when he heard them talking. Now he looked from one of them to the other. When Francesca went into her room, he followed her inside.

She crouched down on the floor with Shadow and wrapped her arms around his neck.

When Grady finally turned and left, she felt like crying.

Shadow licked her chin and she held on to him tightly. When she left, she was going to miss him.

Chapter Four

All night Francesca had tossed and turned, thinking about Grady's kiss. If she was honest with herself, she hadn't just been thinking about it—she'd been reliving it.

The smell of coffee and toast, the sizzle of eggs in a frying pan wafted into her room as she opened the door after her morning routine. She was going to feel awkward with Grady, no doubt about that. Then she thought about the fact that she wasn't wearing a bra because she couldn't hook it. Thank goodness she'd had Grady gather sweatshirts. There were so many things she still couldn't do for herself. But there were so many things she *could* do, too. She could manage.

Shadow had slept with her again last night, and early this morning Grady had opened her door to let him out. She'd pretended to be asleep.

When she'd shared an apartment with Darren, living together hadn't been like this. At the end of their relationship, any time they'd spent together had been fraught with tension. But it was a different kind of tension than she felt with Grady…because *here* she almost felt at home.

That feeling practically panicked her. From experience she knew sharing a home with a man eventually hurt. Sharing a home with a man always came to an end.

When she stepped into the kitchen, Shadow woke up from his nap in front of the fireplace and came to meet her. After she bent to pet him, she straightened. Her gaze collided with Grady's and neither of them seemed to be able to turn away. Then the eggs in the cast-iron frying pan began smoking.

"I hope you like your eggs well-done," she joked.

He grimaced. "I like them over easy, but not black on top. Are you interested in one?" he asked with a wiggle of his brows.

"Do you know how to make poached?" she teased.

He scowled. "I understand eating healthy, but you're eating for two."

Yes, she was. "That's why I'm going to have yogurt, granola and fruit."

"And maybe a scrambled egg?" he suggested.

He was trying so hard. She had to admit she liked that. She liked *him.* She hadn't had many people in her life who had pampered her. Not until Tessa and Emily had come along. And now Grady.

"What are you thinking?" he asked, his voice going gentle.

"I'm thinking that you're being good to me."

"Why wouldn't I be?"

She was saved from answering by the chime of the doorbell. The caller didn't wait for Grady to come to the door to answer it. It opened and a beautiful young woman, possibly in her late twenties, pushed it open wider with her knee, her arms full.

"Hi," she called brightly, making her way into the kitchen as if she knew the house well. She looked at Francesca and then smiled even brighter. "I'm Laurie, Grady's sister. I brought some things I thought you might like—my own trail mix that's all natural and a cranberry-apple fruit salad." She looked shyly at Francesca. "I also brought photo albums. There are some good shots of Grady."

Grady's sister really was a beauty, her wavy black hair tied back in a ponytail, her crystalline-blue eyes lighter than her brother's. She was wearing a yellow down jacket, and white acrylic fur framed her face.

"Did Mom send you?" Grady asked, sotto voce.

"Of course not. I wanted to meet Francesca myself." After she laid everything on the counter, Grady's sister came over to Francesca and extended her hand. "It's good to meet you," she said, sounding as if she meant it. "Grady hasn't told us very much, so we have to see for ourselves. I don't want to make you feel awkward or anything, but the whole family is interested in you and your baby. We want to help however we can. That's what we're here for."

Francesca absolutely didn't know what to say. This was a stranger offering her help.

"I think you've shocked her," Grady suggested, half joking, half serious. He set the platters of food on the table and motioned for them all to sit.

"Is there enough for a third?" Laurie asked.

"Sure is. I always make more, hoping Francesca will eat it."

"Is the baby very active?" Laurie asked, sitting at the table.

Francesca took the chair across the corner from her. Shadow settled at her feet as she answered Laurie's question. "He seems to be getting more active every day. Maybe it's because I'm a neonatologist, but all the charts I've always used, the sonograms I've seen, all the explanations I give to parents mean so much more to me now. At this stage he's already a little person."

"I have two little boys, three and six," Laurie explained. "I still take out their sonogram pictures and look at them. I like to compare what they were then and who they are now. That's why I keep so many pictures around, I guess. Mark, my husband, can't quite understand it. He thinks the albums are good enough. But I want to memorize both of them at every single stage and never forget. Do you know what I mean?"

"I know exactly what you mean," Francesca assured her softly. "In theory, anyway. You want to keep the happy times in a special pocket and pull them out whenever you need them. And the photographs aren't just for you, I'm sure. They're for your kids, too. They need those pockets full of fun pictures. Every child deserves to have too many happy moments to count."

Grady was studying her curiously and she was afraid she'd said too much. "Grady told me you live in Sagebrush in one of the new sections over on the east side."

"We're in a town house for now. Maybe in a few years we'll be able to buy a house."

"I told you if you need a down payment—" Grady began.

"You know Mark and I want to do it on our own. After Seth goes to kindergarten, I'll see if the optometrist I used to work for still needs help. Mark works at the post office," she told Francesca. Then she glanced over at her brother, who was almost finished with everything on his plate. "Did your mustang arrive yet?"

"Sure did. Vince brought her over yesterday."

"Do you know Vince?" Francesca asked Laurie.

She nodded. "There was a storm when he was chief of police here. He helped coordinate cleanup in our neighborhood. He did a great job of it. I got to know him a little bit then because we had a power line down in our yard. I take my kids to his wife, Tessa. Since you're a doctor you probably know her."

"I used to live with her," Francesca replied with a laugh. "She and I were housemates, and then Emily Diaz moved in with us. But since Tessa reunited with Vince and Emily married Dr. Jared Madison, I'm alone there. That's why your brother offered to give me some help for a few days." She didn't want Laurie to think this was a permanent arrangement.

Laurie leaned closer to Francesca. "I was really surprised when he said he was bringing you to the ranch. He never invites anybody but family here."

"Laurie..." Grady warned.

"Well, you don't."

"It's not as if I have a lot of spare time."

The two women exchanged a glance. Laurie was the one who piped up, "Men don't need a lot of spare time to have a little fun. At least that's what *I've* heard."

Francesca told herself not to look at Grady. Don't look at him. Yet her gaze skidded around the table, right to his plate and up to his face. He was staring at her, too. They were both thinking about that night in the saddle shop. Had they had fun? Or had there been too much heat, too much passion, too much intensity to call it fun?

Laurie must have realized she'd insinuated something she shouldn't have. "Oh, sorry. I didn't mean to set my foot in it. I don't know anything about how you met, or how—" she waved her hand in the air "—you got pregnant."

Grady pushed his plate back and stood. "And you're not going to know. That's private." He glanced at Francesca. "The problem is, my family doesn't understand the meaning of the word *private*. They think they can poke their noses in wherever they like. Since you're here today," he addressed Laurie, "is John coming tomorrow? And maybe Liam the next day?"

"Don't be silly. Besides, Liam's having all that fun. I'm sure he wouldn't even think about making you trail mix."

Grady laughed. "I'm sure he wouldn't. But he and John both will want to see the mustang."

Francesca could tell Grady might complain, but he loved his family. How would it feel to have a family like that? She simply had no idea.

"Let's go over to the sofa and look at the albums," Laurie said to Francesca, heading there herself, albums in her arms.

Francesca realized she'd eaten more than she usually did as she'd listened to Grady and his sister. "I'd love to look at the pictures. Especially any you could blackmail Grady with."

Both of them chuckled as Francesca followed Laurie to the sofa. Francesca made sure Laurie was on her right side so she could hear her better. Shadow, coming over to join them, hopped up next to Francesca, though he did look over to his master to see if that was acceptable.

"You're going to go wherever she goes, aren't you? There's no point in my protesting," Grady decided.

"He's not allowed on the furniture?" Francesca asked.

"He wasn't allowed on the furniture until you came. I'll just have to make sure he washes off in the pond a little more often."

Laurie bumped Francesca's good arm. "He's kidding you. He gives Shadow a bath once a week. You should see him in the old washtub out in the barn."

"That could be fun to watch."

"No one watches when I give Shadow a bath. If anyone wants to be there, they have to help me and end up all wet just like I do."

Francesca held up her cast. "I can't get this wet. I'll have to take a rain check."

Laurie giggled and opened the first album on her lap, pushing it over so Francesca could see it, too.

Twenty minutes later Francesca had laughed herself silly at Laurie's stories, as well as some of the pictures.

Grady's sister was full of anecdotes of how the boys had always gotten into trouble and how she'd wanted to join in, but they wouldn't let her. As they went from photo to photo Francesca realized what each represented…a happy family with two loving parents and children who adored them. She saw pictures of holidays—Thanksgiving, Christmas, Valentine's Day, Easter, the Fourth of July, even Halloween. There were many in front of a local church that the whole family attended. There were also photos from school programs, recitals and graduations. No one in this family missed anything.

Francesca's father had missed her whole life. Her mother had only started truly living a few years after they'd left him. But her living had been on a very small scale. She'd always been afraid to try something new, always afraid they wouldn't have enough money, always afraid Francesca would blame her for not having a father. Francesca didn't blame her mother for that. But she did blame her for not helping her feel safe. She blamed her for not acting more like an adult than a child. Francesca had always felt *she* had to be the adult. *She* was the one who had to make the decisions. *She* was the one who had to make sure they were okay. At the end of her mother's life, Francesca had been the caretaker, just as she'd always been. She had been the advocate, the one to hold her mother's hand and tell her it was okay to let go.

These family pictures were affecting Francesca in a way she hadn't been affected in a long time. Doors to her heart began to creak open. She usually didn't think about her past. She tried to dwell on what *was* rather than what used to be. That's how she'd gotten through her childhood and med school and sitting by her mother's bed when she was dying.

Laurie closed the last album. "We have a big gap in Grady's pictures. He was away at college and then lived in Chicago.

"Chicago?"

"I worked there for a number of years before I came back to Sagebrush."

Francesca's gaze sought his. "What did you do?"

"I worked in an investment banking firm for a while."

She felt as if she'd had the wind knocked out of her.

Laurie grinned. "He doesn't seem like the type, does he?"

Francesca remembered the silk shirt. He must have lived differently in Chicago. Light-years from his life here. "Why did you leave it?"

"I'd had enough."

If that didn't cover a world of reasons, she didn't know what did. He'd had enough of Chicago? Enough of banking? Enough of a woman, perhaps? That would be something to ask Laurie when she had her alone.

On the other hand, she could just ask Grady.

"Do you want me to leave the albums?" Laurie asked.

"No," Grady grumbled while Francesca answered, "Yes."

Laurie laughed. "Well, that's a consensus. I'll leave them until the family dinner on Sunday. You can bring them over then." She turned to Francesca. "How long are you staying?"

"Sunday."

Laurie looked down at her arm.

"I know everything I do is going to be limited," Francesca admitted. "Especially at the hospital. But at least I can give instructions if I'm there. I can monitor the newborns with problems, keep an eye on their charts and vital signs. I can do more than just call and find out how they are."

"Can you drive?"

"My car is being repaired. For the first week or so I'll catch a ride with someone if I can."

"Well…" Laurie looked from one of them to the other. "I think I've worn out my welcome for today. I'd better get home to the kids. Mark has some errands he wants to run and it will be easier without Mark Jr. and Seth tagging along." She smiled at both of them. "I'm glad I stopped by today."

Grady didn't respond, but Francesca answered, "Me, too. It was good to meet you."

Laurie actually looked as if she might want to give her a hug. But they really didn't know each other. They weren't family and they weren't friends, although Francesca suspected they could be. On the other hand, maybe Laurie was just friendly because Francesca was carrying her brother's baby. Maybe the family wanted to have no doubts that they would have time with the newest addition to the Fitzgerald family.

Crossing to her brother, Laurie stood on tiptoe and kissed his cheek. "I'll see you Sunday," she reminded him.

He gave her a hug. "Tell Mom I might be later than

usual. I want to spend some time with the new horse. She's going to need a lot of gentling."

"I'll tell her," Laurie said as she opened the door. Then with a wave she was gone.

Grady shook his head. "She comes on strong. I'm sorry about that."

"She was great. Besides, how else would I have gotten to see you in a diaper when you were six months old?"

When he came toward her, she patted the seat on her right. Shadow was still settled in on her left.

Grady lowered himself beside her. "You know, our baby might have your brown hair and your green eyes."

"That never entered my mind," she responded.

"Because he's a boy?" Grady asked.

"I guess." She ran her hand over one of the albums on the coffee table. "Your family looks so happy."

"You sound amazed. Families always take pictures when they're happy. That's why you only see smiling pictures in the album."

She leaned back a little. "You mean you weren't happy?"

"I'm not saying that. I'm just saying the squabbles aren't in there. The arguments aren't in there. The I-hate-yous and the I-never-want-to-see-you-agains aren't in there."

"But none of that matters if you come together again. If you make up, if you see each other's differences and if you're still friends after all that—besides being brothers and sisters—that's because of how your parents raised you."

He must have heard the weight of the sadness in her voice. "Are you going to tell me about your childhood?"

"It wasn't like yours. I don't talk about it. There's no point."

"Frannie—" He lifted her chin with his thumb. "There *is* a point to sharing. When you're ready."

She knew he wouldn't understand. He'd think she was partially at fault. He'd think they should have stayed together as a family and somehow worked it out. He'd think so many things. And that would get all muddled up with the idea of them having a baby.

"What's bothering you?" he asked.

Bothering her? She didn't let the past bother her. That's why she worked so hard. "Nothing's bothering me. I'm glad your sister came over. But now do you know what I'd like to do?"

"Do I want to guess?"

"I'd like to see the mustang."

He studied her for several long seconds. "All right, but bundle up. It's cold out."

When she rose to her feet, he rested his hand on her shoulder. "I realize you changed the subject. Someday I hope we'll have a talk about *your* past…someday when it will mean something to both of us."

If she told him about her past, she'd be giving him a part of herself. She definitely wasn't ready for that. Maybe she never would be.

Francesca took her down jacket from Grady's closet, but then realized she couldn't zipper it one-handed.

"What's wrong?" he asked, ever observant.

"Nothing's wrong. I'm ready."

He was wearing a ribbed red thermal shirt with a navy insulated vest on top. His Stetson and boots added appeal she'd never felt for a man before. As he approached her, her breath hitched.

He took the bottom two ends of her jacket, threaded the zipper into its track and zippered it up to her neck. His fingers were so very close to her chin. "You don't have a hood. Do you have a hat? We're going to be outside to see the mustang and the wind has some bite today."

His voice was husky and she wondered if his breath hitched when he was close to her, too.

Digging into her pocket with her good hand, she produced a green knit cap. But then again, putting it on one-handed could be a problem. As she tried, it slipped to the side and almost fell.

Grady caught it. "Just *ask,* Francesca." His eyes twinkled with amusement as he set it on her head and pulled the sides down over her hair. His fingers seemed to linger a bit and slide to a few other strands. If she leaned forward, her lips would be mere inches from his.

She remembered the happy family pictures she'd examined earlier. Everything about Grady was so magnetically appealing—from his very blue eyes to the dream of the family she'd never had. But the sheer seduction of all of it made her even more afraid to get involved with him.

Leaning away, she took a deep breath. "Let's go see your mustang."

After they left the house, Shadow running ahead of them, they strolled down the walk, crossed the gravel lane and headed into longer grass near the barn.

"Watch you don't turn an ankle. We have jackrabbit holes."

Francesca was indeed careful as she walked. She didn't want to have to grab on to Grady. She certainly didn't want him to carry her back to the house. Her dependence on him was going to come to an end sooner rather than later.

"Look at her," Francesca marveled as she spotted the pinto pony running across the field.

"Since Vince brought her over, she runs and runs. But she doesn't try to get out. I think maybe something's telling her there's safety here, as well as captivity. She nuzzled one of the other horses through the fence yesterday. That's a good sign."

Francesca could see that the mustang's pasture was fenced off from the one beside it.

"She came within three feet of me this morning," Grady confided. "I'm hoping later today, or maybe even tomorrow, she'll come a little closer. Once she trusts me, I think we'll be great friends."

The wind whipped Francesca's hair around her face and she knew Grady wasn't just talking about the horse. "Trust is precious, but it's such a fragile thread. Once it's torn, it's hard to weave it back together again." She felt Shadow against her leg, quietly watching the horse, too.

"Can I ask you something?" Out here in the wide-open spaces with the wind tossing anything it could, Francesca felt a freedom she didn't feel when she was enclosed in a room with Grady.

"You can ask. Depending on what it is, I might decide not to answer," he replied.

She felt her cheeks start to heat a little, in spite of the cold beginning to numb the rest of her. "When I told you I was pregnant, you said the condom you used had been in your wallet for a long while."

"Yes, I did," he agreed warily.

"Did that mean you hadn't been with a woman for a while?"

Grady kept his gaze on the mustang, one hand on the fence. "That's what it meant."

"So…that means one-night stands aren't a habit?"

Now his gaze left the mustang and settled on her. "No, they're not a habit. Are they for you?"

"No! I told you, I hadn't been with a man for a year." She wished she knew why Grady didn't take her at her word.

The wind ruffled leaves on the live oaks. Tall grasses bent to it. After a few prolonged silent moments, Grady asked, "This is the guy who asked you to move to Lubbock?"

"Yes. I was living in Oklahoma when I met Darren Whitcomb at a medical conference. We dated long-distance for a few months and had lots of phone calls. Eventually I moved here and in with him."

"Why didn't it work out?"

"That's water under the bridge," she decided, turning to watch the mustang again. The horse had stopped running and was aware of the two of them standing at the fence. Her ears were perked up and she was listening.

Grady's hand cupped Francesca's elbow. "Why don't you want to tell me?"

Facing him again, she asked, "Are you going to tell

me every detail of your last relationship?" Her instincts were good and she knew he wouldn't.

He blew out a breath. "No, I guess not. But on the other hand, you have seen pictures of me in a diaper."

Grady had a way of using humor to get past her defenses.

The mustang suddenly ran toward them, stopped abruptly and threw up her tail. Grady stood perfectly still and so did Francesca.

"What's she doing?" Francesca asked.

"Trying to make up her mind about us."

Francesca stood fascinated as the horse trotted closer, spun away, ran in a circle and then faced them again. Her dance of sorts continued until she was about seven feet from the fence. Francesca was almost as intrigued by Grady as she was with the mustang. He was perfectly still, not moving a muscle.

Then she heard him say gently, "Come on, girl. I won't hurt you." He slipped something from his pocket and held it out in the palm of his hand.

The horse eyed Francesca.

"What should I do?" she asked quietly.

"Nothing. Just stay still. She's probably afraid if she comes close to me, you're going to toss a rope around her neck."

Holding her breath, Francesca watched as the horse came within two feet of Grady, eyeing the piece of carrot in his palm. Then with a toss of her head and a whinny, she spun away and ran across the field once more.

Francesca was disappointed for the horse. Instinct told her Grady would take good care of her.

Grady stuffed the carrot back into his pocket. "That was closer than before. I'm making progress."

"Will she come inside if the weather turns nasty?" She could see the mustang's corral narrowed, led under the barn's overhang and into a stall.

"She'll come in eventually. She'll let me near her eventually. It's just going to take some patience." After he watched the mustang streak across the pasture, he asked, "Do you want to see the others?"

"Sure."

He studied her face to see if she meant it, then nodded and took her arm to guide her through the tall grass and stones that led to one of the barn doors. It opened with a loud creak.

Francesca was so aware of his arm in hers, aware of his height, aware of his broad shoulders, aware of everything about him. She made conversation to distract herself. "Do you take care of all of this?"

He chuckled. "No. The son of a friend works here after school. Liam helps with any repairs that need to be done. Since John lives in Lubbock he doesn't get out here much, but if I need him, he comes. Laurie rides, so when she can, she exercises the horses with me. Dad used to drive out here more, but I think being here makes him sad because he can't run the ranch himself now."

When they stepped into the barn, Francesca watched Shadow trot down the walkway. She inhaled musky, damp smells of horses, years-old wood and hay. Grady led her to the walkway between the stalls where Shadow sat waiting.

Grady stepped up to the stalls and introduced three horses to her.

Francesca reached out and let the pewter-gray horse smell her fingers as Vince had taught her, then rubbed the side of her neck.

"She's getting her winter coat. I need to let them out for a run and then groom them."

Although Grady hadn't given a hint of it, Francesca knew she was taking up a lot of his time when he should be working or doing chores.

"I can go back to the house on my own." She turned to go.

He caught her good arm. "You don't have to leave yet."

"If I weren't here, what would you be doing?"

"I'd probably be in at the shop. This break is kind of nice. I'm getting things done around here I've let go. I've got a pile of wood that needs to be split. I'm going to tackle that this afternoon."

She could imagine him splitting wood, his face to the sun and his muscles moving under his shirtsleeves.

"I have another question for you," she said softly.

He turned toward her, all of his attention focused on her. "What?"

"Is your sister naturally that friendly?"

"I don't understand."

"I'm carrying your baby. Would your family be interested in me, or even stop by, if I weren't?"

After a few moments of thoughtful consideration, he answered, "You *are* here because you're carrying my baby. But if you're asking if my family would want to meet anyone I was involved with, the answer is yes.

Laurie wasn't pretending interest. She's not like that. Neither is Mom." He paused for a moment. "I'd like to know why the idea of family caring is so foreign to you."

She could deny his conclusion. She could tell him why. But ever since the accident, ever since he'd picked her up at the hospital, ever since she'd felt almost comfortable in his home, she'd wondered if she'd fallen down a rabbit hole. She'd wondered if she was trying to make fantasies become reality. She had to go home, get her life back and look at all of it realistically.

So to Grady she said, "Not today." If he was really patient he wouldn't push her. If he cared, he'd try to develop a bond of trust between them.

Did she really want that? Did she want to get closer to Grady?

He had a question of his own. "Is this a test?"

When she didn't answer, he added, "Because I don't like tests. I like games even less. You and I have to understand each other if we're going to parent together."

Parent together. That's what he cared about. He cared about his son. Well, so did she. "No games, Grady. But sometimes a test or two is necessary before trust can develop. And sometimes trust takes years."

She left him in the barn with that thought, knowing even time couldn't heal some wounds. She might feel the pull of family here. Yet she couldn't forget Grady's main focus was his son.

Their son.

Chapter Five

Late Friday morning, Grady swiped the grooming brush over one of the horses—Avalanche—glancing Francesca's way. Her cell phone beeped, echoing in the stone and wood barn. She'd been restless and, he supposed, feeling cooped up, so he'd suggested she come out to the barn for a little while. She was ensconced in an old captain's chair, a saddle blanket tucked around her for additional warmth, Shadow on a hay bale close by.

Avalanche sidestepped in his stall as her cell phone beeped again.

Grady was glad for the interruption. Having her watch him work had become distracting!

She managed to pull the phone from her pocket and checked the ID. "It's the hospital," she explained.

He unabashedly listened as she answered the call.

"What's up, Josie? Give me the details," Francesca requested a few moments later.

Grady realized Francesca was now in *doctor* mode.

As she listened, he finished grooming Avalanche and left his stall.

Francesca checked her watch. "I'll find a way to get there. Call me on my cell if anything changes."

"*How* are you going to get there?" Grady asked as soon as she closed her phone.

"Can I use your truck? If not, maybe you could drop me at Tessa's and she can drive me. I'll call her—"

Suddenly he was worried and stopped her before she could call her friend. "You can't drive the truck. What if your control with one hand isn't as good as you think it is?"

"Grady, they need me there. The doctor who's covering for me can't be there. His wife is sick and his daughters need him. But there's a preemie with jaundice who's also having breathing problems. What if that were *our* baby?"

"That's not fair," he grumbled.

"Life isn't fair. But I want to make it just a little better for this boy and his family."

"You are one stubborn woman," he announced, half in frustration and half in admiration.

Francesca drew herself up to her full height, letting the blanket fall. "If I were a man, you'd be calling me confident rather than stubborn." She turned and headed for the barn door, Shadow jumping off the bale to follow her, before Grady could make further objections.

If she thought he was going to let her drive herself, she was mistaken. He strode after her and caught up to her as she was putting her cell phone to her ear. "I'll drive you to the hospital."

She closed her phone and stared at him a few seconds, obviously gauging what she wanted to do. Without her cap her hair blew in the wind. The urge to run his fingers through it, to take her to his bedroom and keep her there was so strong that he clenched his hands at his sides.

Finally, she asked, "There's no point in my saying you don't have to drive me, is there?"

"Nope. No point at all."

"Thank you," she acquiesced, giving him a soft smile that aroused him so fast he felt as if his blood was on fire.

He was suddenly grateful winter had come early.

Grady cut a glance at Francesca as he drove her to Lubbock. His overwhelming desire to take care of her was making him crazy. He'd never felt quite this way about a woman before.

He couldn't forget watching her at the fence with the mustang yesterday. She hadn't been around horses much, yet she'd understood the type of stillness that was needed to encourage the wild horse to come close. Most people wanted to reach out to the wilder ones and thought the animals should understand their eagerness to be friends. But Francesca had apparently realized that no amount of reaching could entice such a creature to her. Only stillness and time and patience could establish a bond.

Francesca had been patient with the mustang. And he had to be patient with her. She was very much like that wild horse, although he hadn't realized it the first night he'd met her. She put on a good show, but underneath she was afraid of getting close.

He eyed her again. She was staring out the side window, a distracted look on her face.

"Do you worry about each of your patients this much?"

She glanced at him. "I have to. I have to give them a chance to take their next breath, or beat an infection or develop normally so they can live a full, healthy life. The infant mortality rate in this country is way too high. I try to do everything I can to bring it down."

Infant mortality rate. That phrase sent a chill through him. He knew he'd taken this pregnancy way too lightly up until now. Maybe it was time he faced reality and the risks, along with what he and Francesca had to do to parent this child together. He'd thought taking one day at a time was enough. But maybe it wasn't.

He was as distracted as she was on the rest of the drive to the hospital.

Ten minutes later he pulled up under the portico, quickly got out and went around to her side to help her down.

Before she took his hand, however, she said, "You don't have to stick around. This could take a while. I'm sure I can get a ride back with someone."

"I'll wait."

"Grady, it could take hours!"

"I'll give my dad a call. He can drive over and maybe we can have coffee. As a member of the hospital board, he's here on and off. Don't worry about me. I won't get bored."

She eyed him as if she didn't believe him. Then, apparently deciding there was no point in arguing, she placed her hand in his and let him support her until she stepped to the ground.

They were very close…within kissing distance. Heat spread through him again. Their interlude together on the sofa in his office flashed in his mind. Something about this woman sparked his libido.

In Chicago, his ex-fiancée had been all about her career. She'd been so passionate about it, she'd been unfaithful to him. Not only unfaithful, but she'd betrayed him. She'd slept with their boss to get a promotion Grady had been working for for two years. The worst part of it had been she'd expected him to take it all in stride. As if what she'd done was a matter of course. That's when he'd known he wanted to return to Sagebrush and its small-town values, to a family that was loyal no matter what. He'd suddenly gotten a different perspective on his high-powered career. Sexual attraction had led him to believe there was a connection between him and Susan. But they hadn't put any time into the relationship. They'd just conveniently slept over at each other's places. They hadn't faced life—the low points and the high points—together. Their lives had been mutually exclusive.

It hadn't been easy to leave Chicago without looking back. And now, five years later, at age forty-four, he'd gotten his priorities straight. But that didn't mean he'd forgotten how deceptive a woman could be. That didn't mean he'd forgotten how all-consuming a woman's career could be.

Although he was so tempted to pull Francesca closer and kiss her, he restrained that impulse. Stepping back, he said, "I'll come up to the neonatal unit in about an hour to see how you're doing."

Her cheeks flushed a bit—as if she'd been as aware of him as he was of her—and she nodded. "Just stop at the nurses' station. They'll tell you where I am."

When Francesca disappeared through the sliding glass doors into the lobby of the hospital, Grady stared after her in turmoil about the path ahead of them both.

Grady had been at the hospital for two hours when he spotted Tessa at the NICU nurses' station. "Are you back to work?" he asked, surprised, because Vince had told him his wife wasn't going to return until February.

"Not officially," she replied with a smile, pushing her long, blond hair over her shoulder. "But the doc who's taking my place had some questions about one of my patients who has recurring problems. I stopped in to look over the chart."

"And ended up here?" Pediatrics was in another wing.

"The mom of one of my other patients just had a preemie."

"You doctors are addicted to work, aren't you?" He was beginning to see how Francesca's work could have an effect on their child's life.

Tessa frowned. "No, we're not addicted to work. My children are at home. Mrs. Zappa returned from her visit to her son's, and now she'll be there when I need her to help me with them."

Rhonda Zappa had been Vince's housekeeper before

he married Tessa. She'd taken care of his little boy. Grady knew the couple trusted her implicitly.

"I guess I can't compare this to an investment banking job," Grady admitted.

Tessa laid her hand on his arm. "I don't know. How much did you care about your clients? There are doctors who put in their hours, go home and don't think about their patients. But Francesca and I aren't like that."

Both of their gazes shifted to the double doors of the NICU.

Tessa added, "Francesca cares about each one of those babies as if they were her own. She saves their lives, Grady. Each one of those infants has a hold on her heart."

"She's supposed to be resting," he grumbled.

"I think she's had enough of resting. I spoke with her last night and she's restless to go home."

"She doesn't realize how difficult that will be with her arm casted."

"I think she does. She's already arranged for a ride to the hospital on Monday with Gina Rigoletti."

After a long pause that became awkward, Tessa asked, "How much do you want to be a dad?"

"I think I've been waiting my whole life to be a dad. I called my father this morning. He came over and we had coffee. He talked about raising us, the difference between raising boys and girls. He's been a great role model. I've also watched my brother and sister with their kids. I've got to admit I've been a bit envious at times."

Tessa's blue eyes twinkled. "So now you'll have *your* chance at it."

"I hope so. Francesca and I have to work that out."

"You will, especially if you put your baby first. It will help if you and Francesca can agree on the basics."

"We haven't really settled on the kind of custody we'll have."

"Then there are all the little things, too. Can you stop in whenever you'd like or are you going to adhere to a strict visitation schedule? If *you* have the baby, can she call and ask if she can put him to bed with you? Do you want to start a college fund? Will she consult you if your little boy needs braces?"

He had to admit he hadn't thought of any of the concerns Tessa had mentioned. "I guess a lot of what we do depends on what kind of relationship we have."

"I guess it does."

Tessa was studying him curiously and he felt uncomfortable. He wasn't sure himself what kind of relationship he and Francesca had.

Suddenly the doors to the NICU slid open and Francesca stepped out. Spying the two of them, she crossed to the desk. She and Tessa embraced and Grady could again sense the strong bond between the two women as they began to chat animatedly.

"I can leave now," Francesca said. "Dr. Saxby will be here shortly. And Dr. Martin will be back from his vacation tonight."

"Did everything go okay?" Grady wanted to know.

"For now, but it's still touch and go."

"How about some lunch at the Yellow Rose Diner before we go back to the ranch? Tessa, you're welcome to join us." He thought it might be interesting to hear what the two women had to say when they were together.

Tessa shook her head. "No, thanks. I promised the kids I'd watch a Christmas movie with them. I'll be heading home, too." Tessa returned the chart in her hand to the stand behind the desk. "I'll see you two around. Have a good lunch."

After Tessa headed down the hall, Francesca asked Grady, "Did you get hold of your dad?"

"Yep. We were in the coffee shop for about an hour. He was going to drop in on the chief of staff."

"He knows Dr. Gutieras?"

"They went to school together. I think that's how Dr. Gutieras corralled Dad to be on the board. He wanted a commonsense person."

"That's your dad?"

"Most of the time."

They walked down the hall together to the elevator. When they reached it, Francesca pressed the button for the lobby.

"So, what about lunch?" Grady asked again.

"You really don't need to be anywhere?" she asked, looking worried.

"The saddle shop's doing fine. Christmas orders have come in so everyone's working steadily. I'll have time to exercise the horses and do some chores this afternoon. A half hour for lunch won't throw a wrench into those plans."

She studied him for a few seconds.

"What?" he asked, feeling a bit unsettled.

"Do you always take everything in stride?"

"I had about fourteen years of running like a rat in a maze. When I returned to Sagebrush, I decided I was never going to live my life like that again."

"That was one huge life change."

"Yes, it was, but it was worth it. I'm always going to make time to be a dad, Francesca. You should know that."

He wasn't sure if that statement pleased her or worried her as the elevator doors opened and they stepped in. He still didn't know Francesca, did he?

Maybe he never would.

The Yellow Rose Diner was a Sagebrush landmark. When Francesca had moved in with Tessa, she'd found it a gathering place for everyone, from the town's lawyer to its patrol officers. The restaurant bustled as usual as Grady escorted her inside. Christmas wreaths heaped in a stack by the row of windows threatened to topple onto the pile of red ribbon rolls in the corner.

Grady hung his Stetson on one of the hat holders on the wall, then helped Francesca out of her jacket and pushed her chair in for her. She looked up over her shoulder to murmur thank you and found her face very close to his. She swallowed hard.

After a moment of heart-stopping awareness, he straightened and went around to his seat. He ran his hand through his hair before he settled in across the table.

Francesca remembered running her fingers through his hair. What had happened to her that night? What had happened to Grady? Why had they felt free to be that intimate with each other? Now the tension was ratcheted to such a level between them she could hardly catch her breath. Maybe because the stakes were much higher.

"It looks as if they're decorating for Christmas,"

Grady observed, obviously trying to make conversation. "I usually put up a tree."

"Do you?" That surprised her. Most bachelors wouldn't bother.

"My nieces and nephews tell me it's not Christmas without a tree. They believe Santa might not stop by if he doesn't have a place to put the presents."

She laughed. "Christmas *is* all about children, isn't it? And the stars in their eyes. Tessa and Vince will have a wonderful Christmas this year with Natalie and Sean. Emily showed me the Cinderella coach ornaments she bought for their twins when they were at Disney World for their honeymoon. Courtney and Amy are going to love them."

Grady gave a crooked smile. "Children do make it special. My dad still reads *The Christmas Story* every Christmas Eve. It's a tradition. With his grandchildren gathered around him, it seems to have an even deeper meaning."

Francesca wondered if she'd see Grady over the Christmas holidays. Maybe when she left his ranch, they'd go their separate ways again until the baby was born. Wasn't that what she wanted?

Francesca's favorite waitress came hurrying over to them then, looking harried. Mindy lifted her pencil from its perch in her auburn hair and stood poised to take their order. "Hi, Francesca. Grady. What can I get for you?"

Francesca realized that today the waitress didn't have spare minutes to make small talk. She ordered turkey salad and a glass of milk. Grady ordered a beef club and cheddar cheese fries.

As Mindy rushed off, he studied Francesca for a few moments, then asked, "When you were growing up, did your family decorate much?"

She knew he was trying to see into her past and in a certain sense, she was still ashamed of it. That scared little girl inside would never forget the weight of her father's disapproval, the resounding harshness of his yelling, her mother's cowering fear.

Chatter in the busy restaurant swirled all around them. Maybe Grady thought conversation would be easier here than when they were alone together somewhere. But her past wasn't easy conversation no matter where they were.

"We had one of those electric candles you could plug in and set in the window. Mom put that out every year."

"You said your parents separated?"

"My mother left my father. They never actually divorced."

"Did you see him after you left?"

"No."

Grady stayed quiet as if he were attempting to get a handle on her childhood.

To keep him distracted from the subject of her past, she offered, "I decorated for Christmas with Tessa. That was a lot of fun in the Victorian. We even hung strings of lights outside."

His gaze told her he knew her change of subject was deliberate. He took their conversation in a different direction. "I know you'll be going home Sunday. But how would you like to have dinner with my family first? When I had coffee with Dad today, he said he'd like to meet you."

Dinner with Grady's family. Her curiosity about them, about the dynamics between brothers and sisters and parents had only swelled in the wake of his sister's visit. "Who will be there?"

"Everyone," he answered with a grin.

Everyone. Did she have the courage to take on the Fitzgerald clan?

Sure she did. "What can I bring?"

"Just yourself."

Somehow she'd manage to make a cherry cobbler. She should be able to handle that.

Much easier than she might be able to handle Grady's family!

On Sunday, Francesca's heart thumped hard as she walked into the Fitzgerald one-story condo attached to another on the side street of a fairly new development in Lubbock. Cars spilled from the driveway along the curb.

When Grady opened the door, the aroma of baked goods wafted out ahead of a wave of chatter from the inside.

Francesca glanced at Grady. How many Fitzgeralds *were* there?

He leaned close and whispered in her ear, "None of them will bite. I promise."

She'd tried to hide the fact that family made her jittery, but wasn't very good at it. In fact, with Grady she couldn't seem to hide much at all.

There were three women in the kitchen, all involved in some aspect of the baking process. Maureen was rolling out cookie dough on a pastry cloth. Laurie was removing cookie sheets from the oven. Another woman, pleasantly plump, her hair styled in a pixie cut, was mixing water and confectioner's sugar in a small bowl.

Grady's father, a ruddy-faced, tall man with black hair like Grady's but with silver at his temples, pushed himself up from his recliner and came to greet them. "You must be Francesca," he said with a hint of gruffness in his tone.

"Yes, I am."

Two little boys ran from the hallway and wrapped their arms around their grandfather. Francesca wondered if they were Mark and Seth, Laurie's sons.

"Hey, everyone. This is Francesca." Grady waved a hand at her and pointed to the man at the left side of the sofa. "That's John." He pointed to a younger man at the other side of the sofa. "And that's Liam. Jenna, John's wife, is stirring the icing."

Everyone gave Francesca a nod or smile except Liam. He sort of shrugged and cocked his head, examining her as if she were an alien. At least that's the way Francesca saw it. Grady's brothers hadn't stopped by to see the mustang as he'd expected. Because they didn't want to intrude?

Maureen called from the kitchen, "Come help us with this last batch."

"Let her get her coat off, Mom, before you put her to work," Grady teased.

His mother took it in stride and just gave him a grin and a wink. "Put her jacket in on the guest-room bed with everyone else's."

Francesca felt like a deer in headlights. She handed

Grady the cherry cobbler, shrugged out of her jacket, then traded with him.

A little girl of about five, who had been drawing at the coffee table, came over to Francesca now and looked up at her expectantly. "Are you Uncle Grady's girlfriend?"

Francesca dropped down to her eye level. "I'm your uncle's friend. What's your name?"

"Marly."

"It's nice to meet you, Marly."

The small child eyed Francesca's rounding figure. "Daddy told Mommy you're going to have a baby."

"Yes, I am...at the end of February." Francesca smiled at the blue icing on Marly's chin and a streak of yellow on the front of her T-shirt. "Were you helping to make the cookies?"

"Yep. But I got tired of doing that. But maybe I can show you how to do the angels' wings."

"Maybe you can. Let's go ask your grandma." Francesca stood and followed Marly into the kitchen.

There she handed Maureen the cherry cobbler. While Grady had spent most of the day at the saddle shop yesterday, she'd baked. "I wanted to contribute."

Maureen said, "Thank you. We can always use more dessert. Beef barbecue is simmering in the slow cooker. I didn't add brown sugar since you were coming. We thought we'd be further along with the cookies by now, but cookie-making can't be rushed."

Francesca felt awkward, unsure of what to do or say. But then Laurie piped up, "Francesca lives in Sagebrush in an old Victorian. Tessa Rossi used to be her housemate."

Laurie went on to explain, "Tessa was on call at the hospital one time when Mark Jr. fell off his skateboard. I liked her and started taking the kids to her." Turning to Francesca again, she added, "My Mark and Seth were the two hooligans who ran to Gramps when you came in. Marly belongs to Jenna and John. Their two boys are in the garage trying to fix an old bike."

Jenna offered Francesca a bottle of food coloring. "Do you want to mix the colors?"

"Pink for the angels," Marly piped up. "White for their wings, blue for the bells and yellow for the stars."

"She has it all planned," Jenna said with a smile. "Life's choices are a lot less difficult when you're five."

Francesca smiled back. "I suppose that's true." She picked up one of the small dishes of icing and shook in a couple of drops of blue food coloring. She'd never decorated cookies before. This might even be fun.

After a few minutes of silent work, Maureen commented, "Grady said you went into the hospital on Friday. How did that go?"

Francesca decided if Laurie and Mrs. Fitzgerald had been bluntly honest with her, she could be with them, too. "It felt great to be back. But it was frustrating. Without two hands, I couldn't do what I usually do."

"I can only imagine," Jenna sympathized. "I broke my arm in a biking accident two years ago. I work in the office at the denim factory, nothing like you do. But it was such a relief when I had that cast off and I could feel useful again. I hated not being able to button the kids' shirts or tie Marly's shoes. I can only imagine how you felt at the hospital."

"What do you do at the denim factory?" Francesca asked, eager to move the conversation from her to Grady's family.

"I'm an account manager."

The conversation seemed to roll easily after that. Francesca found she liked decorating Christmas cookies with Marly's help. Maybe Christmas traditions were something to think about planning for the future.

When Francesca glanced into the living room, Grady was cross-legged on the floor with his two nephews, playing some kind of board game. He looked up and his gaze met hers. Was he thinking about how she fit into the Fitzgeralds's Christmas traditions?

Dinner itself was noisy and informal. Mr. Fitzgerald set up a card table for the kids in the living room. Francesca had never experienced anything like this. The adults just fit around the dining-room table. They all held hands and said a prayer before they ate.

She did notice the only one who didn't participate as much in the conversation and laughter was Liam. Grady had told her he'd been divorced recently and she wondered if that was why. Grady definitely favored his father. Liam, with his reddish-brown hair and freckles, favored Maureen.

Since Grady's dad was on the board at the hospital, he and Francesca had much to converse about. They were just discussing the merits of an expanded cardiac rehab facility when Liam asked Grady, "So when are you and Francesca getting married?"

Silence blanketed the table. Even the children in the living room were quiet for the moment.

Not for the first time since she'd met Grady, Francesca wasn't sure what to do. Maybe the best thing would be to let Grady discuss whatever he wanted to discuss with his family without her present. Marriage *wasn't* on the table. Her father had forced her mother into marriage when she'd told him she was pregnant. Francesca had vowed that would never happen to her— no man would ever control her life.

Pushing back her chair, she stood. "Please excuse me. I need to use the ladies' room."

She left the dining room and went down the hall, knowing that the powder room would be her sanctuary for at least ten minutes. That should be enough time for Grady to deal with his brother.

When Francesca did emerge from the powder room, Grady was standing right there outside the door. "Are you all right?"

"I'm fine. I wanted to make sure I didn't interrupt anything when I came back in."

"There was nothing to interrupt two minutes after you left."

She told him the truth. "This family stuff is foreign territory for me, Grady. I just didn't want to interfere."

Grady stood toe-to-toe with her, his voice low. "I'm not making excuses for Liam's rudeness, but he isn't in the best of moods these days. When his wife asked for a divorce, he didn't see it coming. She didn't want to try counseling because she'd met someone else. He's still licking his wounds and that's why he's... bristly."

"I understand," she said quickly.

"No, I don't think you do. I love my family. I wanted them to meet you. But what happens between you and me, that's *private*."

She wasn't sure why, but she did feel some relief at his words. "What did you tell your brother?"

"I told Liam my relationship with you is none of his business."

"I don't want to come between you."

"You won't. He and I have had healthy disagreements all our lives. He's the youngest. There's twelve years between us. He's never wanted to take my advice."

"But you've always wanted to give it?" she asked with a small smile.

"For the past few years I've finally learned to keep my mouth shut. Anyway, I know you've probably had enough of my clan for now. I just happen to have a Christmas tree in the barn. Would you decorate it with me?"

"Tonight?"

"Sure. We've got all evening. I'll get you home in plenty of time to turn in early. What do you think?"

Her hand went to her tummy. This was her last evening with Grady. Decorating a Christmas tree with him could become a tradition with their son.

A tradition. She hadn't experienced many of those. "Yes, I'd like to decorate a tree with you."

Grady's blue eyes darkened. His woodsy cologne invited her closer. A burst of laughter came from the living room and he shifted that way.

No matter what Grady said, his family was important to his life. Would they be important to hers?

Chapter Six

When Francesca stared at the tall, broad evergreen Grady had set up in his living room and the low fire burning in the fireplace, a multitude of feelings washed over her. She realized gratitude and appreciation for today superseded them all.

Grady brought in the last heavy box from the guest room closet and set it on the coffee table. "That's it. Now we can unpack the ornaments and get started."

Get started. She'd begun a process when she'd called Grady from her hospital room. She hadn't realized how involved and complicated that process was going to be.

Curious about the type of ornaments stored in the box, she rose to her feet and went to it as he flipped open the lid. "Are these your family's or yours?"

"They're mine. As you could see, Mom still puts up

a gigantic tree. She kept most of the treasured ones from when we were growing up. Mine are a little more primitive. Many my nieces and nephews have made for me, others I found on travels or were gifts. See what you think."

She peered into the box. The first ornament she lifted out was a miniature angel with a crocheted skirt. The delicate white thread wound about her in rings and was obviously starched. Her wings were the same delicate threading. Her face was a painted wooden ball and her halo was made of gold wire.

"Where did this one come from?"

"The wife of one of my customers. I had a display set up in my shop for her to sell a few of them before Christmas."

"It's wonderful." She lifted out another. It was a leather boot with a gold bell for a spur.

"One of my employees made that one."

Grady was near to her now, near enough that their hips bumped. As they bent over looking into the box, their elbows brushed. Neither of them moved away, and Francesca knew she should.

Taking the angel ornament by its little red string, she crossed to the tree and hung it on one of the branches. This could be the start of a Christmas tradition. Emotion lodged in her throat.

Grady must have been watching her and saw her bite her lip.

Suddenly he was at her shoulder. "What is it?"

"Hormones," she replied with a small, forced smile.

Grady hesitated for a moment and then wrapped his

arm around her shoulders, turning her toward him. "You can only use that excuse once a month for me to buy it."

"First time this month," she joked.

His hand went to her stomach, startling her. "Honesty—for the sake of the baby. Remember?"

Oh, she remembered. Gazing into his very blue eyes, she felt so many emotions. Emotions she'd never had before, never let herself *feel* before. Because of the baby or because of Grady?

"I didn't have a pleasant childhood," she began, the softest way she knew how.

When he removed his hand, she realized how protective that simple gesture had been.

He tilted his head and studied her. "You're going to try to sugarcoat this, aren't you?"

"Most people can't deal with it otherwise."

"No sugarcoating. Just tell me what happened."

"Grady…"

Perceptive, he asked, "Why don't you think I'll understand?"

She studied the angel for a few moments. "Because your family is loving and connected. You grew up with a mom and dad who loved you and protected you. That is absolutely huge."

"Neither of your parents protected you?"

For him to understand, she'd have to paint a picture. "What's your earliest memory?" she asked him.

He considered her question. "I was about three when my dad put me on a horse for the first time. We have a picture, so I don't know how much my memory comes from that or from the event itself. But I recall things that aren't in the picture—the feel of his hand on my back, the way he held the reins, the coarseness of the horse's mane as I held on to it."

She could tell Grady still appreciated every aspect of remembering. She also knew memories were the most vivid when emotions were high. His that day had been the sheer excitement of a new adventure.

Hers today would be the lingering scent of Grady's cologne, the soft feel of his flannel shirt and the intense look on his face as he studied her now and asked, "What was yours?"

"Like you, I was about three. I was hiding in a dark closet as my father yelled at my mother."

Grady stayed silent and she guessed he was hoping she'd go on without his prodding. "I have a lot of memories of hiding in the dark in that closet until I was eight."

His hands slid from her shoulder to her hand and he tugged her over to the sofa.

After they were seated, he said, "He abused your mother?"

"Yes."

"When he came home drunk, you went and hid because you knew what would happen."

"Yes."

"Did it go beyond black eyes and split lips?" His voice was as grim as his expression.

"Sometimes. Sometimes she'd lie in bed for a day or two and I'd crawl in beside her. The one thing I remember most besides the dark and the fear is how helpless I always felt. I wanted to make her pain go away. And not just the physical pain. I saw her tears, and when I was really young I thought they were from the physical hurt. But as I grew older, I realized she was suffering in her heart. Somehow I thought that by putting my arms around her, by staying close, I could help."

"Did he touch *you?*" Grady asked gruffly.

"Not as long as I stayed in the closet."

She didn't know why, but telling Grady about this, about her, was much harder than it had been to tell Tessa, Emily or Vince. Maybe because she didn't want pity from him. She did *not* want him to feel sorry for her. She was past it all now and on to a different life.

"You don't talk about this, do you?"

"No. There's no reason to."

He looked dubious. "There's more to it than what you've told me. You said your mother left your father. How old were you?"

"I was eight."

"What made her finally leave?"

He was still holding her hand and he rubbed his thumb across her palm. Grady was the father of her child and she didn't want to keep secrets from him. She knew secrets damaged relationships and didn't build them.

"It was a Saturday night," she remembered all too well, keeping her gaze on his strong fingers holding hers. "We heard my father come up the steps unsteadily. He fell once and swore. He started yelling before he even reached the apartment door. It was 10:00 p.m. but he said his supper had better be on the table."

She shivered, all of it rushing back although she'd tried to erase the sights, sounds and feelings for years. She went on as if a play were unfolding in front of her eyes. "As soon as my father opened the door, I headed for the closet. But that night I didn't *stay* in the closet. I thought his voice seemed fiercer than usual. When he got louder, I heard something fall. I was afraid it was my mom. I came out of the closet into my room."

She could remember the heat of the floorboards under her feet, the scent of jasmine floating through the open windows, the little bedroom that had been a refuge. "My room was small, only big enough for a single bed. But I had that closet. Two doors between me and my father had always seemed to be better than one. That night, though, I suppose I was tired of hiding. I felt like a coward when I hid. I felt like I should do something to protect my mother."

"You were only eight!" Grady protested, sounding as if just the thought horrified him.

"I was old enough to know the consequences of talking back. My mother had become more passive over the years. If she didn't fight him, she didn't get hurt as badly. But that night, for whatever reason, I couldn't be passive. I couldn't let him hit her again."

Francesca closed her eyes as if that would blot out the pictures. But she knew better. "I watched through the keyhole. When he went for her I flew out of there, yelling for him to keep away. But he came after me instead of her and backhanded me across the face, then again across my ear. I ended up on the floor seeing stars. My mother always had a teapot on the stove. She grabbed it, threatened my dad with the hot water, pulled me off the floor and took me to her bedroom, where she locked the door."

The memories were still so real when she summoned them up. "I expected him to break it down, but he didn't," she went on. "He shouted at us, and then left. When my mom examined me, she saw I had hit the leg of the table when I'd fallen. I had a cut across my temple that needed stitches. My ear was hurting and I couldn't hear on the right side. She dragged a suitcase from under the bed, packed as many of my things and hers as she could shove into it, took money she'd been hiding away from a jar under a floorboard and hurried me outside. We ran a couple of blocks until she flagged down a taxi to take us to the hospital. The doctors treated me and sent us to a shelter. A week later we were on a bus to Oklahoma and a new life."

Grady's expression was filled with so much compassion, Francesca could hardly stand it. She expected the usual questions like, *Did you ever see your father again? How difficult was it starting over? How did your mother handle it?*

Instead, he asked, "How long was it until you stopped being afraid?"

Maybe he *did* understand. "I was in my early twenties. I had taken two self-defense courses in college. That helped. In my late twenties I decided to find out if my dad was still in Salinas. I learned he had died two years before and knowing that wiped out most of the fear."

But she knew there was still a residue. Sometimes it kept her from taking risks.

Grady's voice was gentle. "I'm sorry for what you went through. You're right, it's hard for me to imagine it. I guess anyone who hasn't gone through it can't truly understand it." They sat in silence together, his hand still covering hers. "So has it been hard for you to have serious relationships because of all of this?"

She knew what he was leading up to—and she might as well get this over with all at one time. "I know it might sound crazy, but for a long time I didn't even realize my background was the reason I didn't want to date. I made the decision to become a doctor when I was in high school. I was all about getting good grades, winning scholarships, putting all my energy into my career so that I could make my mom's life better, too. Then in med school I hardly had time to breathe, let alone get involved with a man. But I had that mentor I spoke of—Joshua—who was so kind. He was the first person I told about my childhood. When I did, he warned me not to be too careful because that could lead to mistakes, too. I didn't know what he meant then, but I found out."

"With this Darren you were involved with?"

"Yes. I *was* careful. As I said, I met him at a medical conference. Maybe because I was on my home turf, maybe because I was missing my mother—she'd died the year before and I felt a little lost without that connection—when he asked me to show him around the city on a break, I agreed. We'd had several professional conversations by that point and I liked him. He was charming…without coming on strong. He said he didn't drink. I couldn't find any similarity to my father."

Grady's intelligent blue eyes sparked and he made the connections. "But he was like your father in some way?"

"I didn't see it at first. We had lengthy phone calls

long-distance for a few months. He told me about the Family Tree Health Center opening in Lubbock and said the hospital where he worked was looking for a neonatologist and offices were available at Family Tree. It would be a risk for me to start a new practice somewhere I'd never been, so I came down to visit for a few days and he showed me around. Sure there was some arrogance about him, but I've found that's often the case with doctors, so it wasn't surprising. There was…an attraction." Though nothing like she felt with Grady! But she wasn't about to tell him that right now. Everything was too raw and vulnerable for her to be even more vulnerable with him.

"So you packed your bags and moved here?"

"I did. I became friends with Tessa almost right away. We consulted on a case, had lunch and I…connected with her. Thank goodness I did. As soon as I moved in with Darren, he began becoming more possessive. When I wasn't working, he wanted to know where I was every minute. He didn't give me Tessa's phone messages if she called the condo. I started having nightmares again, nightmares like I hadn't had in years."

"Nightmares about being locked in a closet?"

"Yes. Then I realized why. I was starting to feel trapped, as trapped as I'd felt as a little girl. With our work, Darren and I didn't have a lot of time together. We snatched dinners when we could and managed to get away one weekend. But when I returned, I had a new little patient who was hanging on by a thread. I was at the hospital day and night for a week. Darren understood his own dedication, but sometimes I don't think he understood or believed in mine. Whenever I mentioned I was interested in learning about neonatal units in other hospitals—which could involve traveling—he shut down the conversation completely."

She saw Grady's frown, but he didn't interrupt her. Now she just wanted to finish. "One morning, Darren told me he wanted to go to dinner with me that night and he'd made reservations. I explained I'd already made plans with Tessa. His reaction was over the top. He got angry, took me by the shoulders and shook me, telling me I was having dinner with him. I was so shocked, I couldn't say a word. Then he left, slamming the door behind him. As soon as his car sped out of the driveway, I packed my bags and moved in with Tessa. I swore off ever getting involved in a relationship again. I turned my back on dating and poured everything I had into my little patients."

After a long pause, Grady said gruffly, "But then you went to an open house."

Yes, she had. When she'd met Grady, she'd felt giddy and excited, forgetting everything that had gone before. "I really don't know what happened that night, Grady. My life was in gear again. I was happy…busy. I was living with two good friends and had everything I needed. I wasn't looking for—"

"For a roll on a denim couch? No, neither was I."

"Then…why me?"

"Have you ever looked at yourself in a mirror?" he asked wryly.

She felt heat suffuse her cheeks. "I'm sure there are lots of pretty women around here."

"You were more than pretty. You were smart. You

didn't try to make me notice you. We just started talking. Every time we ran into each other that evening, we talked some more. You were easy to understand. You knew how to listen. You didn't seem to like that crowd any more than I did. But I never expected what happened in my office to happen, either. That wasn't my motivation for asking you to go there. I mean, sure, I was thinking maybe I'd like to take you to dinner sometime. But whatever flared up between us caught us both by surprise. It was too hot to escape."

Just sitting here like this with Grady, she could feel the heat again. She could feel the buzz of electric attraction every time she looked at him, every time he touched her, every time they exchanged a word.

Now when he leaned closer to her, their chemistry together tempted her, enticed her, coaxed her to believe this man was different from all the others. His lips on hers were gentle until the heat took over once again. It consumed them both.

Grady's mouth was so sensually teasing. His arm was strong and muscled as it circled her. What was it about him that made her want to jump out of her own skin into his?

She hardly noticed when his hand slipped beneath the hem of her top. But she definitely noticed when she felt his callused fingers on her side. With a fleeting thought, she was so glad she wasn't wearing a bra so there was no impediment when his hand moved higher, when he cupped her breast and his thumb circled her nipple. She moaned and pressed into him, needing more, yet at the same time, she wanted to give more.

Grady's hand on her breast urged her to reach for

his shirt and pull its fabric from his jeans. The growl in his throat when she touched bare skin led her to fumble with his belt buckle. In no time she had it open along with his fly. Sliding her hand inside his briefs, she caressed him until he broke their kiss and held her face between his palms.

"Frannie!" His voice was deep and husky. "Do you know what you're doing?"

"The same thing you're doing," she returned, the sensual haze between them lifting a bit, though their breathing was still short and shallow.

"I don't want to take advantage of you."

Were her defenses down because of what she'd told him? Had his kiss been full of pity and compassion and she'd thought it had been more? How could she have just tumbled into this with him again?

She slid her hand away from the intimate contact. She let her defenses once again weave their fingers around her heart. Physically, as well as emotionally, she withdrew from him.

"Don't look at me like that," he protested.

"Like what?"

"Like you're sorry you told me anything."

Maybe she was. Because now she felt more vulnerable than she ever had before. Sometimes secrets were terrific insulation against the risk of loving and the pain when everything fell apart.

When she leaned away from him, his hands dropped from her face. She straightened her sweatshirt, took a deep breath and didn't look at him again until he asked, "You *are* sorry, aren't you?"

She wasn't getting into a revealing conversation again. Just because Grady was a good listener, just because there were sparks between them, didn't mean he really cared about her. He cared about his child, but that wasn't the same thing at all.

"Maybe I should go home now. Gina's picking me up tomorrow morning at seven-thirty."

"How are you going to get home from work?"

"I have several options. Don't worry about me, Grady. I'll be fine."

His gaze was penetrating as he studied her. He must have realized he couldn't persuade her to take more time off. Without embarrassment or awkwardness he zipped up his fly and rebuckled his jeans. "You have my number if you need it." The tightness in his tone was not lost on her.

She would call him if something happened that involved his child. Otherwise, she wouldn't be calling Grady until she went into labor.

As Francesca opened the front door of the old Victorian a half hour later, Grady was right behind her, carrying her suitcase. She was vitally aware of his physical presence. She had been since they'd almost made love in his living room.

Silently, he followed her inside. She went in, turning on lights as she went.

He stayed in the foyer. "Should I leave your suitcase here?" he called.

Seeing that everything on the first floor was still as it should be, taking in a breath of the old house and the

For Busy Women Only!

You deserve it!

Mail this card for your:

✓ FREE BOOKS & GIFTS
✓ Time-saving quick reads
✓ Step-saving home delivery
✓ Sanity-saving "just for me" treats

Scratch off the gold circle to see the value of your 2 FREE BOOKS and 2 FREE GIFTS. We will send them to you with no obligation to purchase any books, as explained on the back of this card.

We want to make sure we offer you the best service suited to your needs. Please answer the following question:
About how many NEW paperback fiction books have you purchased in the past 3 months?
❏ 0-2   ❏ 3-6   ❏ 7 or more

335 SDL EZV9   235 SDL EZWL

FIRST NAME   LAST NAME

ADDRESS

APT.   CITY

STATE / PROV.   ZIP/POSTAL CODE

Visit us online at www.ReaderService.com

The Reader Service - Here's How It Works:

Accepting your 2 free books and 2 free mystery gifts (gifts are worth about $10.00) places you under no obligation to buy anything. You may keep the books and gifts and return the shipping statement marked "cancel." If you do not cancel, about a month later we'll send you 6 additional books and bill you just $4.24 each in the U.S. or $4.99 each in Canada. That is a savings of 15% off the cover price. It's quite a bargain! Shipping and handling is just 50¢ per book.* You may cancel at any time, but if you choose to continue, every month we'll send you 6 more books, which you may either purchase at the discount price or return to us and cancel your subscription.

*Terms and prices subject to change without notice. Prices do not include applicable taxes. Sales tax applicable in N.Y. Canadian residents will be charged applicable provincial taxes and GST. Offer not valid in Quebec. All orders subject to approval. Credit or debit balances in a customer's account(s) may be offset by any other outstanding balance owed by or to the customer. Please allow 4 to 6 weeks for delivery. Offer available while quantities last.

SEND 2 FREE
BOOKS &
2 FREE GIFTS

BUSINESS REPLY MAIL
FIRST-CLASS MAIL   PERMIT NO. 717   BUFFALO, NY

POSTAGE WILL BE PAID BY ADDRESSEE

THE READER SERVICE

PO BOX 1867

BUFFALO NY 14240-9952

NO POSTAGE
NECESSARY
IF MAILED
IN THE
UNITED STATES

If offer card is missing, write to: The Reader Service, P.O. Box 1867, Buffalo, NY 14240-1867 or visit www.ReaderService.com.

light cinnamon scent of potpourri, she returned to the foyer. "Yes, just leave it there."

His brow furrowed. "I *could* carry it upstairs."

Yes, he could. But her dependence on him was over. "It's okay. Really."

He shoved his hands into his pockets.

Francesca knew she had to slice through the tension, but wasn't quite sure how to do it. "Thank you for inviting me to your house this week. The truth is—I've never had anyone look after me that way."

As he studied her, the lines around his mouth didn't cut quite so deep. "I guess that's why it was so hard for you to relax."

"I relaxed," she protested.

"When I wasn't around."

He really *was* on the mark. They couldn't seem to be around each other without generating…something—something that was incendiary and dangerous and she knew would eventually hurt them both. They had no basis for a relationship beyond their attraction and this pregnancy.

He added, "I'd still like you to let me know how you're doing, how you're feeling. Will you do that?"

"I will," she assured him, knowing now he really cared about her welfare.

He proved that again as he moved toward the door and asked, "Do you have food in the house?"

"Enough. I'll get some groceries tomorrow."

To his credit he didn't ask how she would get those groceries.

Her phone rang.

"You'd better get that," Grady said, and stepped outside.

"Thank you," she called after him.

But he just tipped his hat and strode to his truck.

Her phone rang again. As she closed the door, she turned to answer it. She swallowed around the lump in her throat. Was she upset because Grady was leaving?

She was startled to see Darren's number on the caller ID. Why would Darren Whitcomb be calling her at home?

Anxiety tapped at her chest as she picked up the phone and told herself there was nothing to be afraid of. She'd left Darren. It was over.

"Hi, Darren."

"Hi, yourself. I tried to call earlier. I heard about your accident and I wanted to know how you were."

Did he know about the baby, too? Probably. Hospital scuttlebutt was faster than Amtrak. What he didn't know was whose baby it was. No one had known that except for Tessa, Vince, Emily and Jared.

"It was kind of you to call, but I'm fine."

"I heard one of the nurses say you came in Friday to take care of the Vasquez baby, but that you weren't returning to your own house."

Why would Darren care if she was at her own house? "I stayed with…a friend. My physician thought that was better after the accident. One of my arms is in a cast for at least a month and I'm getting used to that."

"But you're coming back tomorrow?"

"I'm going to see how it goes."

"You're always the conscientious one, aren't you?"

His voice was too familiar, as if he knew her better than he did. "Aren't all doctors?"

"Not in the same way. You know that."

She kept silent, waiting for the reason for his call. They hadn't ended their relationship on friendly terms. He'd been angry she'd left. She'd just been so relieved to be away from someone who wanted to control her, someone like her father, that she hadn't cared if they remained friends or not. But they did work in the same hospital—although on different floors and without much direct contact—so they should take a stab at being civil. Was that what Darren was doing?

"I have a case I'd like to discuss with you, a young pregnant woman with tachycardia. Would you have time to have coffee with me sometime tomorrow?"

"Darren, why aren't you asking Dr. Saxby or Dr. Martin?"

"Because we work in the same hospital and I think it's time we get over what happened. There's no reason why we can't be friendly colleagues."

Francesca hated the fact that she was suspicious, but she didn't believe that Darren did anything without good motivation. What was his motivation for this? Or was she just being paranoid? Still, she wasn't a coward and if he wanted to have a face-to-face meeting she would do that, though it might be their last.

"I'll have to assess my day when I get in in the morning. Can I give you a call around nine?"

"Nine is fine. Then we can set up a time to meet."

If she set up a time to meet—

Her doorbell rang. Had Grady forgotten something? Her heart started an excited little patter.

"Is that your doorbell?" Darren asked. "It's getting late for visitors."

That was his "I know what's best for you" tone. She'd better get off the phone before she said something she shouldn't. "Yes, it is, so I'd better see *who* it is. I'll give you a call in the morning. Have a good rest of the night, Darren."

"I'll talk to you in the morning," he agreed, and hung up.

Francesca thought over the puzzling conversation as she went to her door, looked through the peephole and spotted Tessa standing on her stoop. Her arms were filled with two bags.

She called, "Let me in before I drop these."

Francesca laughed and opened the door. Tessa hurried to the kitchen and set the bags on the eat-in counter. "I thought you might need supplies. Or did Grady take you to the grocery store?"

"No. I was going to shop tomorrow."

Something in Francesca's voice must have alerted Tessa as to her distraction. "What's wrong?"

"What's wrong? You mean besides having an accident, gestational diabetes, being taken care of by Grady for almost a week, meeting his entire family and then getting a call from Darren?"

"Darren? What did *he* want?" Tessa started emptying the bags. She knew where everything went.

"I'm not sure. He says he wants to meet for coffee to talk about a case."

"But?"

"But he and Dr. Saxby have been colleagues longer

than he and I have. And Dr. Martin is back from vacation. Darren and I haven't spoken since I left him."

"Maybe he wants closure."

"Maybe."

After Tessa stowed milk in the refrigerator, she studied her friend. "So how did the week go?"

"I saw you on Friday."

"Yes, you did, but we couldn't talk with Grady there."

This was Tessa, her friend. She didn't have to watch her words or worry about their meaning. After she took a loaf of bread from one of the bags, she put it into the bread keeper. "He confuses me, Tessa. Everything that happened before and is happening now between us confuses me."

"Why?"

"Because there's too much feeling attached to the air when he's in the same room!"

Tessa laughed. "And that's a bad thing?"

"That's a bad thing if neither of us wants to be personally involved."

Tessa's eyes cut to Francesca's baby bulge. "I think you're beyond personally involved."

"You *know* what I mean. Beyond being parents together. I'm not even sure I want to do that. I'm not sure about anything except that I love this baby already and I only want to do what's best for him."

"That will probably mean having Grady in his life."

"I suppose so. It's just that we're so very different. You know what I came from. He's satisfied to be back in Sagebrush and doesn't want to live anywhere else. I've always wanted to see more of the world. Just because I have a child doesn't mean I can't do that." She paused, then added, "Tessa, I just… I don't trust him. I can't."

"You don't trust men in the generic sense. Grady is one man. One awfully rugged, handsome Texan, don't you think?"

Francesca groaned and dropped her face into her hands, with her elbows on the counter. "I don't believe in fairy tales, remember? So don't start weaving one."

"I think Vince and I, and Emily and Jared, have found our happily-ever-afters. Why don't you think *you* can?"

"Because there are too many obstacles to overcome, too many memories I'd have to wipe away, too many doubts that are always with me. No man would want to take them on. And Grady? I think he has walls of his own. Even with that terrific family of his."

"Do you know anything about his life before he settled in Sagebrush again?"

"Not much. Just that he was an investment banker in Chicago. His sister told me he was all set for a promotion and then something happened."

Francesca raised her gaze to Tessa's again. "He gave up that life and now he could really focus on raising a child. Maybe he's being nice to me just because of the baby. I have to be careful about that."

"You don't think he'd try and take physical custody away from you?"

Francesca's heart practically stopped at the thought and a chill crept up her spine. "You never know. I don't want to give him grounds. But I also want to live my life in a way that's best for me and the baby. I don't want to have to worry about his approval or disapproval."

Tessa crossed to her and put her arm around her. "You don't have to make all the heavy decisions tonight."

Francesca glanced sideways at her.

They both smiled. "No, I guess I don't," she said.

But she knew she was going to have to make major decisions...very soon.

Chapter Seven

Francesca sat across from Darren in the café at the Family Tree Health Center the following afternoon, comparing him to Grady in spite of herself.

Both were good-looking men, both had an air of confidence about them. But after that the comparisons ended. Darren's hair was cut short and neat. His curious gaze now even held some interest. She didn't want that interest.

They'd talked about one of his cases for a good fifteen minutes, but now he pushed the folder aside. She realized the conversation was going to shift to the personal when he said, "You're looking good."

"I'm feeling good. And if we're finished talking about your case, I really have to be going."

"Important date in the middle of the afternoon?"

He'd tried to keep the question light, but there was

an edge behind it. She'd learned how to read that edge. It took root in the fact that he wasn't in control and he didn't like it.

"If by a date you mean an appointment, yes, I'm going to look at day-care facilities."

"With the baby's father?"

She could shoot back that that information was none of his business, but she kept her tone neutral. "No, with a friend." She pushed back her chair.

"Tessa Rossi?"

As she stood, she felt defensive and she replied bluntly, "Darren, it's really not your concern."

He acted nonchalant. "Just trying to make friendly conversation."

She thought about all the friendly conversations they'd indulged in at the beginning of their relation-ship...even the first month she'd moved in with him. But then friendly had transformed into these questions with the edge underneath. He'd been suspicious of where she'd gone, what she'd done and with whom she'd done it. Their comingling lives had become about *his* schedule, *his* cases, *his* upward climb at the hospital, *his* likes and dislikes from movies to restaurants. She'd found she was losing herself. Finally when he'd laid his hands on her in anger, the scared little girl inside her had pushed out of her closet and run for dear life.

Suddenly Darren seemed to realize he'd reverted to an old pattern. "I just want to know how you are, Fran-cesca. When I heard you were in an accident, I was worried. Just because we split up doesn't mean I stopped caring."

When Darren was his charming self, he *always* wanted something. She didn't know what he wanted now, but she wasn't going to wait around to find out.

"Thank you for your concern, but I'm fine, really. And I have to be going."

With another forced smile, she rose and headed past the ledge lined with pothos ivy and a bird-of-paradise potted plant...out of the café. She was escaping again. She knew that. But wasn't that the best route to take?

At the doorway she turned left and practically ran headlong into Gina Rigoletti. "Gina, I'm sorry. I was distracted."

"You *look* distracted. Actually, I was searching you out. Somebody told me you'd come down here. I wanted to make sure Emily was still picking you up and you didn't need a ride home."

"She's still picking me up."

Gina studied her. "Are you okay? You look a little pale."

Everybody was asking her if she was okay. She appreciated their concern and their kindness, but all of it was becoming a little unsettling. So she told the truth. "I just had a consultation with Darren Whitcomb about a patient. But he and I were involved once and it was a little unnerving."

The two women had started walking along the sunny yellow walls. Gina stopped in a small alcove with two leather chairs that looked out a plate-glass window over the grounds. "Even the thought of exes can be unnerving," she said solemnly.

Francesca gave her a questioning glance. She knew

Gina had moved back to Sagebrush not so long ago, and she was staying with her parents.

"Do you have a few minutes?" Gina asked.

"I have about fifteen unless I'm paged."

That morning Gina had seemed distracted on their drive to Family Tree, but Francesca hadn't asked questions. They'd had several conversations and were becoming friends, but she didn't want to poke into private areas.

Francesca took a good look at Gina now. She was a beautiful young woman with black curly hair. Head of the baby development center, she was an expert in her field and mostly spent her time working with children who were developing more slowly than they should be.

Gina looked hesitant now. "I wondered—are you looking for a housemate? I just love your Victorian house. I know you had housemates who moved out."

"I didn't think anyone would want to live with a new mother and an infant!"

"I work with infants and toddlers. I love them. I wouldn't mind that at all."

"Even the interrupted sleep?"

Gina laughed. "Well, let's just say my dad snores and my mom has insomnia. My sleep has been interrupted since I returned to Sagebrush."

Francesca liked Gina. She also missed Tessa and Emily.

"I'd understand if you need to think about it—" Gina ventured.

Instinct made the decision. "I don't need to think about it. When would you like to move in?"

A grin broke across Gina's face. "I brought up the

subject with Mom last week about finding my own place. She and Dad would really like me to stay through the holidays. So why don't we say the first week in January?"

"That sounds great." Francesca checked her watch. "I think my fifteen minutes are up. We can talk about this more tomorrow."

The unexpected happened more often than not. As she and Gina went their separate ways, the possibility of finding a new friend in Gina made her smile. She'd have to introduce her to Tessa and Emily.

On Friday afternoon, Francesca waved to Tessa as she drove away from Laurie's duplex. Grady's sister had phoned her and asked if she'd be interested in baby furniture her kids no longer needed. Francesca had told her she'd stop by after a doctor's appointment with the endocrinologist Tessa had driven her to. Laurie had offered to drive her home.

Francesca hated depending on others. But that concern was miniscule compared with what the diabetes specialist had reminded her of. Gestational diabetes could lead to premature delivery or an overly large baby. She had to take care of herself down to the letter. More exercise for one thing. She was going shopping for a treadmill tonight even if she had to do it online!

To her surprise, before she could even ring the doorbell, a truck pulled up to the curb. It was Grady's!

She waited to push the bell. As he approached, she asked, "What are you doing here?"

"Laurie called me. She thought you might need someone to lift and carry."

Was his sister playing matchmaker? Had Grady told Laurie that Francesca might push him out of her life?

Instead of ringing the bell or opening the door, he commented, "I heard you were visiting day-care centers."

"You heard? How?"

"Sagebrush is a small town. One of my customers saw you going into Wee Care Day Care."

"And he or she ran back and told you? How did they even know you were the father?"

"I'm not keeping it a secret. Are you?"

"No, but I've always kept my private life private. I don't put it onstage for the whole world to see."

And they both knew why that was. She'd learned the lesson well from her mother.

"Frannie, my customers have been my customers for years. Many of them are friends."

Whenever he used her name like that she felt all warm and melty inside. Then she thought about her conversation with Darren on Monday and how their relationship had ended so differently than it had begun. Why would she think Grady would be any different? Wasn't he demanding some sort of control now?

"Did anyone also tell you I went to Little People's Day Care and Rainbow Day Care in Lubbock, too?"

He frowned. "No. Why so many? Why any at all? If we had talked about this I could have told you—" He stopped when he saw her expression. "What?"

"I scouted out facilities because I knew they might have waiting lists, and they did. Do you expect me to discuss my every step with you?" She knew she sounded defensive. She knew she might even be picking a fight.

But she didn't want to feel trapped, or watched over and especially not controlled.

Grady gently took her by the shoulders and looked into her eyes. "Whoa. I don't know what you're thinking, but I suspect it isn't good. If you had told me, I could have mentioned that Laurie knows the woman who runs Rainbow Day Care in Lubbock. She has great credentials. But she doesn't take on babies until they're at least six months old."

"I know. That's why I'm also looking at other options. Vince and Tessa's housekeeper/nanny, Mrs. Zappa, is wonderful. Vince found her through a service. I was thinking of maybe going that route." The heat from Grady's hands warmed her through and through. Maybe he didn't want control. Maybe he just needed to be involved.

"I have another suggestion." His face wasn't very far from hers. "My mother said she'd consider minding our baby if you went back to work."

Francesca didn't know what to say to that. Grady's intense blue eyes staring into hers stirred up deep emotions, and she still didn't know why.

"Taking care of a baby would tie her down," she murmured.

"I don't think she'd care—she offered. But you can talk to her yourself about it if you're interested."

Was she interested? Did she want to become even more entangled with Grady's family?

"I know what you're thinking. You don't know if you want me or my family in your life."

She'd never thought she was so obvious. But with Grady— He saw behind the walls and the excuses.

"We can't act as if we're a couple, because we're not," she protested, leaning away.

He released her shoulders and stepped back. "No, we're not. And I can see your point. But if you want to go back to work, you have to find someone you can trust."

"I want to think about it."

"That's fair." He put his hand on the doorknob.

Impulsively, she clasped his arm. "Grady…I told you about my background and it wasn't easy. At some point I'd like you to tell me about yours."

He dropped his hand to his side. "You already know how I grew up."

"I do. But I don't know other things. Were you involved in serious relationships? If you want to be a dad, why haven't you ever married?"

He tipped down the front brim of his Stetson and she knew what that meant. He was uncomfortable and would rather not talk about it. He hedged. "This isn't the time or place."

"Will there *be* a time and place?" she asked quietly.

"We'll see."

Yes, they *would* see. Because she wouldn't let it go. She felt transparent with him, as if she'd given a lot more than he had. She needed to know Grady's romantic history. She needed to know what had kept him from becoming a family man before now.

"Did you ask her?" Laurie targeted her brother.

"No, I thought I'd let you do that."

Laurie lived in a town house. As soon as Francesca and Grady had walked inside, she'd thrown her question at him.

Seth, Laurie's three-year-old, came running toward Grady full-bore and wrapped his arms around Grady's knees. "Uncle Grady! Uncle Grady! Let's play horsey."

He picked up his nephew and held him high in his arms. "Just a minute, cowboy. I might have to do some talking first."

The little boy wrinkled his nose at him, gave him a kiss on the cheek and then squiggled in his arms to be let down.

Francesca had to smile despite the trepidation. The talking would likely cover his mother babysitting. Maybe both he and Laurie were going to try to convince her.

"Grady told me your mother offered to babysit," she said to Laurie, wanting to be up-front.

"Oh, he did? Well, I guess Mom's disappointed because I decided to stay home with Mark and Seth until they're both in school. Jenna did the same with Marly. I think Mom would have liked to have her own family day-care center."

Laurie glanced toward Seth, who was occupied in one corner of the living room with LEGOs. "No, this isn't about babysitting. I have some baby clothes besides the crib, play saucer and swing. The kids were in and out of them before I hardly had a chance to wash them. They grow so fast."

Francesca had to start thinking about saving for a college fund, and she still had school loans to repay. Everything would change with this baby, especially if she took time off. She'd saved money wisely over the past few years, but that wouldn't last forever.

"Yes, I'm interested. I'd love to see what you have."

"The crib, the saucer and the swing are in the shed out back. They should fit in Grady's truck if you want to take them along."

"I'd like to pay you for them."

"Absolutely not. When you're finished with them, maybe you can find someone else who can use them. If not, I'm sure I can. As long as they're in good condition, we'll just keep passing them on."

"I like that idea."

Laurie motioned to her to come sit on the sofa. "Do you have time to look through the clothes and see what you want and what you don't?"

Francesca's eyes met Grady's. He shrugged. "I have time."

Making time for what he felt was important seemed to be easy for him. Would he do that for his son?

"Those are deep thoughts," Grady said when she hadn't spoken for a few moments.

"Not so deep." She ducked her head to the box and opened the flaps. But Grady wasn't going to let her get away with that.

"We'll talk later."

That was either a promise or a warning.

A small smile played on Laurie's lips as she took in their interchange and opened a second box.

While Grady let Seth climb on his back to play horsey, Laurie went through the clothes with Francesca. She looked through terry cloth play sets, footed pajamas, even a winter bunting that would be just right for the time when her baby would be born. She held up a little shirt decorated with a helicopter and the blue jeans to go with it.

"Not only does Mom like to babysit, she likes to buy baby clothes. I thought I'd warn you before the baby's born, because she'll have a few gifts," Laurie said.

Francesca was absolutely amazed by the generosity of this family. The way they thought about each other and others, the way they worked together, was a stark contrast to her parents and their attitudes and what they'd had and didn't have. "Your family amazes me."

"Because of our sheer numbers?"

Francesca laughed. "Yes, but…also just by who they are. I didn't have a lot growing up, and my mother didn't reach out to others very much. So your generosity just kind of bemuses me."

"*You're* generous."

"Excuse me?"

"You are. Look at the field you've gone into—saving newborn lives."

Francesca ran her fingers over the embroidered duck on an infant shirt. "There's something about a baby that makes the rest of the world good again. I have to do whatever I can."

"I think Grady's afraid to believe you are what you seem," Laurie confided in almost a whisper.

Francesca kept her voice low under little Seth's laughter. "Why?"

"He'll have to tell you that. He's a good guy, Francesca. Being a guy, he can be a little arrogant and patronizing and impatient sometimes. But he's a good guy."

He'd been patient with her. But the uncertainty of visitation rights loomed. Were they the reason he was putting his best foot forward?

That same question continued to nag Francesca an hour later as she stood in the guest room that she'd chosen for the nursery and waited for Grady to bring up the crib.

When he carried it into the room, he stopped and met her gaze. Her breathing came faster. An electric charge filled the air.

"Are you going to leave the walls yellow?" he asked, trying to make conversation.

"I thought I would. I could hang little boy decorations on them."

He chuckled. "You mean like baseballs and footballs?"

"I have some photos of horses and a few catalogs with more ideas. I just haven't gotten serious about decorating yet."

He let that comment hang in the air as he propped the crib against the wall, then went to the tool belt he'd brought up earlier that was lying in the corner.

"Can I help?"

He took a Phillips screwdriver and a wrench from the belt and then approached her. "You can hold on to these. I'll need them once I open up the crib."

She took the tools from him, their fingertips grazing. Her breath caught and maybe so did his, because he froze for a few seconds and then moved quickly away.

Ten minutes later the crib was angled in a shadowed

corner of the room. Francesca stood by, ready with a set of pale blue sheets and a navy-and-white spread. Grady lifted the mattress from its position against one wall and plopped it into the crib. Francesca shook out the cotton sheet.

He watched as she fitted it on the mattress. But she had trouble with the fourth corner.

Without a word, Grady rounded the crib to stand beside her, took hold of the material and yanked it into place. The side of his body was practically smack against hers. She could feel his heat, his muscled tautness as he straightened and didn't step away. She held her breath.

"It's hard to believe that in a few months our baby will be sleeping in this crib." His voice was rough and she could tell the thought affected him deeply.

"Sometimes it doesn't seem real to me, either. But then I just put my hand on my tummy. I'm connected to this little person in a way I've never felt connected before. I feel as if the future has opened up in front of me. Each step will be a new adventure."

"Sometimes I can feel your joy," he surprised her by saying. "It just radiates from you."

She wasn't aware of that. She just knew that at moments she was completely happy and content. Maybe that's what Grady could feel.

He was facing her now. When his arms came around her, she automatically slipped her arms around him. No matter what her doubts were, they were sharing this adventure. This baby was his, too, and she was realizing more each day that she couldn't cut him out of her life.

Standing with her like that, he gave her a slow smile. "The baby's getting bigger."

She felt her cheeks heat. "So am I."

"Not really." He ran his hands slowly up and down her back, sending shivers up her spine. "Your breasts are fuller."

"Grady—"

"Well, they are. I notice things like that, especially since I remember exactly how they looked before."

"Stop," she protested softly.

"Why? It's not as if we haven't been intimate."

Physically. But how connected were they emotionally?

She pondered the question. Yet as Grady's head bent to her and his strong arms grew a little tighter, as she leaned into him more, letting their baby press into him, she knew she was becoming connected emotionally to a man—really connected—maybe for the first time in her adult life.

That realization careened against the walls around her heart. Yet fear hardly had a chance to start because when Grady's mouth captured hers, she felt something much different. Something more than a simple connection. One that could lead only to heartache.

Yet didn't she deserve something more than fear and separation? Didn't she deserve to see a dream in the distance and hope one day she'd find the right road to lead her there?

Grady's hands slid from her back to her waist. He grasped handfuls of her maternity top and lifted it until he felt her skin. She wanted to feel his, too, yet—

What if this attraction was only that for him—an

attraction? What if physical satisfaction was all he was seeking? What if this was simply a means to keep her and the baby close? Did she dare take a chance?

He must have felt her hesitation because his hands dropped away from her midriff…and the baby. His tongue stopped probing and his lips clung only a second before they separated from hers.

He gave them both a few moments to cool down and then he asked, "What are you thinking about?"

"Why you came back to Sagebrush. I also want to know why sometimes you mistrust me almost as much as I mistrust you."

"Maybe you want to know too much," he replied tersely.

"Maybe. Or maybe I have the right to know who the father of my baby really is."

Grady began to unpack the play saucer.

Francesca felt as if the road to her dream had just grown much longer.

Chapter Eight

"That's the last box," Grady said fifteen minutes later as he plopped it on the floor.

Looking up, he was surprised to see Francesca hanging framed photographs of horses on nails she must have hammered in. When she turned, he felt that sucker punch that was becoming all too familiar. Her eyes had the power to do that to him and he didn't like it. He liked it about as much as the personal questions she'd been asking.

"Did you take those?" he asked. "In fact..." He studied the photographs more carefully. "Aren't they Vince's horses?"

"I have a digital camera. It doesn't take a genius to do something like this now. I sent them to be printed in eight-by-tens, found mats and frames and here they are."

"So you were serious about the horses?"

"I'm living in Texas now. Why wouldn't I be serious about horses?"

Maybe he had hoped for a different answer. Maybe he had hoped *his* horses and *his* ranch had something to do with it, because their son would be spending time there.

She was studying him, and he didn't want her to skip from one realization to another. "You need a rocking chair."

"Actually I found one at a yard sale two months ago. Tessa knew someone who refinished furniture and I've been using it in my bedroom. I guess I just wasn't ready to put this room together yet. But now I think my nesting instincts are kicking in. I'll have to buy a chest and a changing table, diapers and bottles, stroller and car carrier. Goodness. I guess I'd better get started."

Now he remembered a rocker in her room. He hadn't paid attention to the furnishings when gathering her clothes for the stay at his place. "Maybe Santa will bring some of the things you need."

"I've never written a letter to Santa."

"Are you serious?"

"I never thought he could give me what I needed. I wasn't interested in toys. I was interested in a real home."

Francesca seemed to be as genuine as a woman got. He was finally learning about the feelings and fears and the hell she'd been through as a child. "Why don't I go get that chair? You can decide where you want it."

"My room's a mess. I wasn't planning on a visitor."

He just touched his hand to the side of his hat as if to say, "That doesn't matter," and headed for the Wedgwood blue-and-white room.

He stood in the doorway this time, having more than a few minutes to take it in. She'd told him she'd brought her furniture from Oklahoma. It was plain, with straight lines and a beautiful wood grain. The room might seem like a mess to her, but it just showed him the evidence that she lived here. Sweatpants and a T-shirt lay over a corner of the bed, running shoes at its foot. The bed *was* made, however. The dresser held a jewelry box, a mirror and a framed photo of an older woman he presumed was Francesca's mother. Other than that it was uncluttered. The white ceramic lamps and white trim around the doors and baseboard lent a pristine aura to the space.

He spotted the rocking chair over by the window. Unlike the rest of the furniture, it was a bit more decorative, with its tall, rounded back and staves for support leading from the top down to the seat. The arms were solid wood and sturdy with spokes leading to the seat also. The planks on the seat were molded in such a way that they looked almost comfortable rather than stiff and unforgiving. The rockers were large and would give good motion. It was an interesting chair, as interesting as the woman who had chosen it.

He lifted it, carrying it to the nursery. He had to decide which of the rooms in his house he would turn into a nursery. Did he want Francesca's input or would he rather do it on his own? He might keep the horse theme, but in a more primitive way. Liam was great at drawing. Maybe he could paint a little cowboy with a rope on one wall and a horse on the other. The more Grady thought about it, the more he liked it.

Bringing the chair into the nursery, he set it by Francesca, who was standing at the window, staring out into the yard. "We'll have to look at swing sets. They have baby seats now that that you can attach to them."

"And a jungle gym for when he's older. Boys like to climb and explore."

She turned. "Girls don't?"

"Oh, no. I'm not stepping into that one!" He examined the room with a critical eye. "Where are you going to find a chest and a changing table?"

"I'm not sure, but I still have time."

They gazed at each other, more quiet than they'd been since she'd asked him her questions.

"I could use something to drink. Got anything in the refrigerator?" he asked.

"Sure. Soda, juice, beer for when Vince visits and wine for Jared."

"A bottle of beer sounds good."

She looked around the room again and smiled. "I'll have to write your sister a thank-you note. This has really helped me get started."

"You don't have to write her a note. Everybody's coming to the ranch this Sunday. I'm going to play Santa. You're welcome to join us. You can thank her then."

"I don't know, Grady. I often work Sundays."

He knew when Francesca was going full tilt she might work seven days a week. "You can't get away for a few hours?"

"Let's see what the weekend brings."

Did she want to see what the weekend brought or did she want to see how much he'd give of himself? He hated talking about the past, and especially about what had happened with Susan, because he felt like such a fool.

A short while later they'd gone downstairs. Francesca poured herself a glass of milk and brought him a longneck beer. They sat on the sofa, silent at first, and awkward together in that silence. They'd been intimate, but not really. They were friendly, but were they really friends? She kept her guard up with him and his past few years of not wanting to get involved with anyone kept him from becoming involved with her. At least in a real way.

He knew why *she* was hesitant. She'd had a rough road. He guessed the worst part of it was that she didn't trust her own judgment now. She was sharing more and he wasn't. The least he could do was to be as forthright with her as she'd been with him.

He didn't know how to start, so he just jumped in. "You asked why I'm not married."

She didn't say anything, just gazed at his face and listened. Her complete attention did something to him. It loosened words that had been stuck in the back of his mind.

"When I went to Chicago, I decided I wanted a life outside of Sagebrush. I'd grown up here. I wanted to make my mark in a big city…see more of the world. And I did. Or at least I'd started to. I was willing to travel and it helped me move up in the firm. I saw Hong Kong, Amsterdam, Geneva, Paris and even New Delhi. A colleague and I started an affair. I thought it was going somewhere. I thought it would lead to marriage and children and a life in Chicago, different from the one I'd seen in Sagebrush, but with the same family values."

"And she shared your values?"

"Well, that's the thing. I thought she did. I thought everyone looked at marriage the way I did, the way my parents did, the way my sister and brothers did. But then the opportunity for a promotion came up and we were both in line for it."

"It's hard to compete with someone you love," Francesca said with understanding.

"I think we could have handled the competition. *I* could have handled the competition. But apparently she felt she needed an edge. She slept with our boss to get the promotion."

"Grady, I'm so sorry." After a pause she asked, "Did she get the promotion?"

"Yes, she got it. The worst part of it was she didn't think she'd done anything wrong. Afterward she told me sleeping with him was just part of the game. It didn't mean anything. I remembered all of the nights we'd spent together and wondered how much *they'd* meant to her."

"How did you find out she'd slept with him?"

"One of my 'friends' told me. He'd seen them together in the boss's office late one night. I didn't want to believe it. I asked her why she'd been there that late, and she admitted that's how she'd gotten the promotion. She didn't just sleep with him once, either. They met at a hotel two or three times, nights I thought she was out with friends or working late."

"You must have felt so betrayed by both of them."

"Betrayed…deceived…used. So I confronted him. As long as that was the way he did his business, I was quitting. The whole thing left such a bad taste in my mouth, I came back here. After I licked my wounds for a few weeks, I decided Sagebrush was where I belonged. I missed my family. I missed the ranch. I missed loyalty, honesty and forthrightness."

"But you lost your ability to trust a woman."

"I absolutely didn't understand how she could say she loved me in one breath, then tell me she slept with a man to get ahead in the other. Those two concepts just don't work side by side. That's when I realized our values were very different."

Francesca was studying him curiously.

"What?"

"But there must have been good parts. Do you ever miss your life in Chicago?"

"People talk about the advantages of big city life, the cultural events, the stores, the employment opportunities. But I don't see it that way. I can find anything I want in Sagebrush. Just give me a good horse, a loyal dog, work I like and my family around me and I'm satisfied."

Francesca bowed her head and looked down at her hands in her lap. She picked up her glass of milk, took a few sips and then set it back on the coffee table on the coaster. "Do you believe what I tell you?" she asked.

"I try to. I try to give you the benefit of the doubt. But the truth is, Frannie, I half expect you'll take our child, move to Timbuktu and I'd never see you again."

He noticed she didn't say she wouldn't do that. The hell of it was, he understood why. If he turned out to be an SOB like her father or like this Darren character, she'd be off without a second thought.

When she turned toward him, her glossy hair fell over her shoulder. He thought about the times his hand had slid into it so easily. The whiff of a clean, spicy floral shampoo scent came with it, and he realized she got to him in a way Susan never could.

Her gaze was wide with doubts as she asked, "Do you really want me to come on Sunday?"

He loved playing Santa for his nieces and nephews. He wanted Francesca to be comfortable with him at the ranch so she'd bring their baby there often. He didn't want her to lock him out of her life. "Yes, I want you there."

She took a deep breath and let it out, as if this was a major decision for her. "All right. I'll make sure I'm not needed at the hospital on Sunday. I'll see if I can arrange it so I can stop in for a while."

"One of my family can pick you up."

He intended to make Sunday convenient for her. But those doubts were back in her eyes. She didn't know what his family would mean to their child. She didn't know if his family would be more than she could handle.

He was going to have to warn them all to back off.

But that could be a hopeless cause.

"Ho, ho, ho!"

Francesca had been standing at the dining-room table at the ranch arranging food for the gathering. Patrick Fitzgerald had opened the front door to his son. All of the children ran toward him, including John's nine- and ten-year-olds. But little Seth, who came running through the dining room at full tilt, tripped and fell.

When he began crying, she realized his mom had gone to the guest-room closet for more napkins. Francesca rushed to him and hugged him. "It's okay. I don't think you're hurt, are you?"

The little boy shook his head. "I want to see Santa."

Francesca stood with Seth's hand in hers and guided him through the living room to the foyer where all the children were gathered with Grady. He was busy shaking hands with the older kids, patting the little ones on the head. But when he spotted Francesca with Seth, his gaze held hers. The intensity of his focus seared a path right down to her toes. She wondered if they could ever just be in the same room together without producing enough electricity to light up his tall Christmas tree.

She stepped forward a little. "Seth wanted to say hello to Santa. I think he was afraid he wouldn't get here in time."

Grady tried to smile under his Santa beard. "Not in time?" His voice was an octave lower than it usually was. "All the children are in time. Let's go into the living room and see what Santa has in his bag."

On the floor behind him sat a huge red bag with drawstrings. In it, he'd loaded candy canes, oranges, bags of gummy bears and puzzles. As Grady ho, ho, hoed his way to the living room with the bag, the adults laughed and followed, too.

Except for Maureen, who sidled up next to Francesca. "I think you're going to make a really good mom."

Surprised by the certainty in Maureen Fitzgerald's voice, Francesca asked, "Why do you think that?"

"Because you didn't hesitate to comfort Seth."

Francesca knew she was good with babies, and she loved kids. But would she make the right choices for her own child? Her mother had gotten trapped in a bad situation because of the decisions she'd made.

"You look troubled," Grady's mother noticed.

They were ten feet away from the fray, children gathered around Grady, parents keeping them corralled, excitement and laughter and Christmas spirit tumbling out of everyone. Francesca didn't have older women in her life to confide in, wise women who knew from experience about heartaches and difficult times. She wondered if Maureen did.

"I'm thinking about my own mother."

"You said she passed on a few years ago?"

"You remembered."

"You and Grady are having a child together, Francesca. I want to get to know you." She glanced at her husband, who was steadying the big red bag so Grady could pull out the treats. "I believe Grady will make a good father because Patrick was a good role model."

"That's my worry," Francesca confessed. "My mother was fearful of many things, my dad the main one. We left him when I was a child. She never learned to be her own person. She never learned to make forward-looking decisions or to take control of her own life."

"You have control of *your* life."

"I'm not so sure about that. My hours are erratic, so in a way I don't have control there, especially when emergencies crop up. And they often do with newborns in peril. Then there's the pregnancy, which I thought I had control over, but the diabetes put a wrench in that."

The older woman's eyes were kind. "You don't need control to make the right decisions. Maybe the best time of life is when fate is tumbling us around and we still manage to get up again."

"I can see why your children are so successful at whatever they do."

"And I can see why *you're* successful. It's the spirit within us that makes us who we are…and what we believe. You're a strong woman, Francesca. I was a little worried when I heard about your career. How would you shuffle responsibilities to deal with pregnancy and the time-demanding schedule of a newborn? But I think you'll figure it out."

"Grady told me about Susan."

Maureen looked surprised. "He did? Well, then, I guess you know it's hard for him to trust. She betrayed him on many levels and I don't know if he'll ever get over that."

That's exactly what Francesca had thought. "This baby is more important than my career."

"Have you told Grady that?"

"I haven't really had the chance. He thinks my career is all I can see ahead of me. It *is* important. It will give this baby a future. That's why I have to figure out a way to juggle it. So I don't lose it."

Maureen patted Francesca's arm. "I think you'll do fine."

Francesca realized the woman's support meant a lot. Because she was a calm wise voice or because she was Grady's mother?

The children were happily playing with their puzzles

when Santa gathered up his empty bag, tossed them a few more ho, ho, hoes and left the house. Francesca knew Grady would be changing back into his regular clothes in the barn. She slipped out a few minutes after he left and ran to the small side entrance. He'd dressed in the tack room.

When she opened the door and went inside, she saw he was still dressed. "Don't you want to stop being Santa yet?"

He turned to face her. "Actually, I was just imagining playing Santa with our son. Next year at this time, he'll probably be grabbing at my beard and yanking on my belt. The toys won't mean much, but the fantasy will start for him."

"I was thinking of next year, too. I guess…I guess we'll be sharing custody."

"Will we?" he asked soberly.

"Is that what you want?"

"I want what's best for all of us. I don't want you to feel cheated and I don't want to feel as if I'm missing out."

"How do we prevent either?"

"I'm not sure yet." Suddenly his mood changed from serious to jovial. He plopped into a wooden chair, grabbed her hand and pulled her onto his lap.

Laughing, she asked, "What are you doing?"

"I'm playing Santa Claus. What do you want for Christmas? And don't tell me a baby in perfect health. That's a given. I'm talking about your Christmas list. What's on it?"

A baby in perfect health. She hadn't told Grady their son could be premature or have other problems. But why alarm him? Why not just hope for the best outcome?

She could tell underneath Grady's laughter he was serious and she thought about his question for a few moments. "What I need most is a desk for my computer. I'll be working at home more after the baby's born and it would be nice to set up a little corner for myself. I can stay in touch with the hospital, receive updates on my patients and know exactly what's going on."

"You want a computer desk? Not a diamond necklace? Or a gold bracelet? Or a new designer purse?"

Leaning against Grady, she gazed into his eyes. Maybe he was unrecognizable in the Santa outfit, but she'd know those eyes anywhere. "Nope, just the desk."

"So you think you'll be working at home more?"

"I've been considering it…doing consultations more than hands-on practice. I don't know what I can arrange and how I'll handle it financially. I need to keep my foot in the water, professionally speaking, and yet I want to spend as much time as I can with my baby…our baby."

His arms around her held her a little tighter and she found she didn't feel trapped. She felt ready for Grady to kiss her again…with or without the fake beard.

Instead of kissing her, though, he said, "I have a solution to your problem."

"What?" she asked warily.

"Move in with me. If you're living with me, we'll both have access to our child and I could provide some of the child care you need, though we might want to have someone come in and help. You also wouldn't have to worry about a roof over your head."

"I'd have to pay my fair share."

"We could work it out."

Could they work it out? Was it what she wanted? Living with the father of her child? Did she dream of more?

No. She couldn't believe in dreams. Not when their child's welfare was at stake. She liked her independence. She liked living in the Victorian. She had been planning to share the big house with Gina.

Living with Grady. Should she even consider it?

"You can't keep this baby to yourself," he reminded her.

"No, I can't, but I do have to live my own life, Grady. I don't know if I can do that if I'm staying with you."

He didn't look as if he accepted that reasoning. The easy humor between them evaporated, and as gracefully as she could, she scrambled off his lap. "We've got to get back to the house or everyone will wonder where we've gone."

"I wonder that myself sometimes." His tone was acerbic and Francesca suspected he usually got his own way.

Not this time.

Chapter Nine

"Aren't you going in?" Tessa asked, a twinkle in her blue eyes.

With Christmas fast approaching in nine days, Tessa, Emily and Francesca had decided to go Christmas shopping Wednesday evening. Emily had met Francesca and Tessa at the Yellow Rose Diner for supper and then they'd proceeded to wander in and out of the specialty shops. Francesca had already found Grady a Christmas present online that she hoped would please him.

Now the three of them were standing in front of his saddle shop.

"He asked you to live with him," Emily reminded her. "The least you could do is stop in and say hello." Her voice wasn't as much scolding as it was teasing.

Francesca had told her friends what Grady had suggested. They'd both remained neutral on the subject. "What are you two going to do if I do stop in?"

Tessa pointed to a bookstore. "I need books for the kids and a biography Vince is interested in."

"If you finish first, come find us," Emily suggested. "If we finish, we'll come find you."

Francesca hadn't spoken to Grady since his family gathering on Sunday. The atmosphere between them had been strained as he'd driven her home. She knew why. He wanted access to his child and inviting her to live with him was the best way to get it.

"I won't be long," she assured them.

"I can spend hours in a bookstore," Tessa said. "So don't hurry on my account."

"Same here," Emily agreed.

After encouraging looks, they headed off across the street.

Francesca composed herself, attempting to appear placid, and opened the door to Grady's shop. Maybe he wouldn't be working tonight. If that was the case, seeing him was a moot point. Yet she realized she wanted to see him and that fact bothered her, too.

The bell over the door jangled as she stepped inside. She hadn't been in the front of the shop before. It was quaintly attractive with saddles on pedestals. Shelves displayed leather goods—from bridles to key chains braided with horsehair to a display of Navajo blankets. No one stood at the counter and cash register to the rear of the display area, but Francesca heard voices not far away—a man's and a woman's. She realized there was a small room off the front area of the shop and didn't know whether to venture into it or not.

Instead, she called, "Hello."

Grady emerged from the small room with what looked like a sample catalog in his hand. "Francesca! What are you doing here?"

A pretty, young woman with strawberry-blond hair, freckles on her nose and a Stetson with a chin tie followed him. She was holding a bridle.

Francesca didn't have a chance to answer his question before he added, "I'll be with you in a minute. I have to add a few things to Cassidy's order."

When Cassidy peered at Francesca inquiringly, Grady introduced them. "Francesca Talbot, Cassidy Dugas. Cassidy, Francesca."

"It's nice to meet you," Cassidy said, then turned back to Grady. "You'll have everything ready by the end of January?"

"At the latest," he assured her. "You want the saddle for your brother's birthday."

There was a note of familiarity in Grady's voice that told Francesca Cassidy Dugas was more than a customer. When Cassidy replied, she was sure of it.

"I want to surprise Jesse, so if he comes in, don't give anything away."

"I wouldn't do that."

Cassidy took some bills from her purse. "How much do you need for the down payment?"

"I usually require half."

The pretty woman's face fell. "I only have a third. I can give you the rest next week when I get paid."

"That's fine." He winked at her. "I know where you live. I can always confiscate that wagon I like so much."

She laughed, and in that laugh Francesca knew they'd been close at one time. She felt deep disappointment in her chest. Maybe it wasn't disappointment. Maybe it was something else she didn't even want to think about.

"I told you, if Jesse ever wants to sell that wagon I'll let you know." Cassidy gave him a smile that was feminine and teasing.

After Grady took her money, he rang up her down payment.

Cassidy waited for the receipt, glanced at Francesca, gave her a nod and then left the shop.

Off-balance at the interplay between Grady and Cassidy Dugas, Francesca stepped up to the counter. She said, "I could have come back later."

Grady didn't comment, but came around the counter. "Have you been doing some Christmas shopping?"

"With Tessa and Emily. They're over at the bookstore."

"And you stopped in to—"

"I stopped in to be…friendly, that's all. But I didn't know I was going to interrupt something."

"You didn't interrupt anything."

She knew what she'd seen hadn't simply been a shop owner and customer relationship. "Did you date her?"

"If I had, would you be jealous?" His eyes twinkled and he tried to keep from smiling.

When she didn't respond, just stood there, purse in hand, he shrugged. "I dated Cassidy a few years ago. Her brother and I were in school together. We went to the movies a few times and then to Lubbock for dinner.

But it didn't go anywhere. She's a wonderful woman, but I couldn't forget about Susan. And Cassidy wasn't…she doesn't sleep around." He crossed his arms over his chest. "I answered your question, now you answer mine."

"Of course I'm not jealous," she blurted out. "Why *would* I be?"

He took the purse from her arm and set it on the counter. Then he laid his hand on her belly, which was getting rounder by the day. "Because I'm the father of your baby. Because, whether you'll admit it or not, you like me just a little."

She finally had to admit to herself she liked Grady a whole lot. If she liked him any more…

She'd be falling in love with him.

No. She would *not* let that happen. She was not opening herself to getting hurt. Dreams like that were as wispy as the morning fog.

Coming closer to her, he clasped her shoulders. "Sometimes, Frannie, you can't hide everything you're feeling."

When he bent his head, she thought about pulling away. She knew she should. Every time he kissed her, their physical attraction blossomed. But the thought of being held in Grady's arms was too tempting to resist. Sometimes she hated being alone. Sometimes she longed for a bond that would last a lifetime. Was that a dream? She hoped not…because she didn't believe dreams came true.

His lips were warm on hers, mobile, coaxing. Everything about Grady was…coaxing. His "Aw, shucks, I'm just a cowboy, I didn't mean to tempt you" attitude was disarming. Somehow his smile, his gentleness and his innate sexiness curled around her defenses until she wondered what had happened to them! Even now, as she was aware of what occurred every time she was near him, that awareness didn't seem to matter. All that mattered was the grip of his large hand on her shoulders, the scent of him—cologne and man mixed with leather—the sensual provocativeness of his lips on hers. Thoughts galloped into that neverland of pleasure.

Pleasure increased when his tongue slipped inside her mouth. That pleasure was a tinderbox of desire. Her hands slid to his waist, tunneled under his leather vest to his flannel shirt. He was hard under that shirt, his muscles honed from ranch work and riding. She ached to really touch him again, to find out if the second union of their bodies could be as good as the first. Yet most men didn't find pregnant women attractive. Many men found pregnancy off-putting.

Pregnancy. Having Grady's baby. Figuring out what was best for their son.

She stilled and Grady slowly ended the kiss. Then he leaned back and studied her. "Now tell me if you weren't just a little bit jealous."

She couldn't hide the truth now. "Maybe I was. Just a little."

He laughed. "Well, I'm glad we got *that* settled. And actually I'm glad you stopped in. I was going to call you when I got home."

"What about?"

"My family always gets together on Christmas Eve. We go to evening Mass and then back to my parents' to exchange gifts. I'd like you to join us."

"I'm going to be on-call Christmas Eve. The hospital's always short-staffed over the holidays."

"If you get called in, so be it. But if not, I think you'd enjoy yourself. We sing Christmas carols and everything."

He added the last so tongue-in-cheek, she had to smile. "Tessa and Emily both asked me to join their families, but I don't think they'd mind if I spent Christmas Eve with you."

He studied her for a few long moments and then asked, "Do you really *want* to spend Christmas Eve with my family? Because I don't want you to do this out of some misguided duty to our unborn child. Sometimes I can't read you, Frannie, so be straight with me."

If she labeled this "duty" she'd be deluding herself. But she hated feeling vulnerable with anyone, and that included Grady. "Did you *invite* me out of duty?"

He shook his head with a wry smile. "You're good. Just when I think I'm making progress—"

"Progress goes two ways."

"I guess it does," he admitted. "No, I'm not asking you out of duty. I'd like you to be there. Laurie and my mother would like you to be there. The more the merrier."

"I want to come, Grady. Yes, I'd like to begin a tradition for our baby, but…" She hesitated, then plunged in. "But I like being with you."

"And that scares you, doesn't it?"

She nodded.

"We could just be parents with benefits," he joked. "Maybe you should think about that."

She had a lot to think about—Grady's sense of duty

and responsibility to his child, their attraction to each other. But she had the feeling Grady didn't let his mind go beyond that, and she shouldn't, either.

Parents with benefits? Sex should be the last thing on her mind right now. Yet when she looked into Grady's eyes her body quickened in response. He threw everything in her life into confusion.

"I'd better go," she murmured, knowing she was running away.

He knew it, too. But he thought she was only running from the chemistry. He was wrong. She lifted her purse from the counter.

"I'll pick you up at six-thirty."

"Six-thirty will be fine."

As she turned to leave, he called, "Frannie."

She glanced back at him.

"Don't think so much."

She couldn't respond, just pulled open the door and left his shop. Thinking was much safer than feeling, she reminded herself as she headed toward the bookstore and her friends.

On Christmas Eve, Francesca sat beside Grady on the sofa at his parents' condo after church services. It was as if they were a couple—yet weren't. Grady didn't touch her in front of his parents. She didn't know how she felt about that. Their relationship wasn't clear, that was true. But she also felt Grady was holding back. They weren't so very different after all.

As the children and adults finished their light buffet supper, Grady leaned closer to her. "I have your present at the ranch. I didn't bring it along. Do you want to stop there on the way home?"

She'd brought his present along. But she wouldn't mind privacy to give it to him. "Would you like to open yours here or do you want to save it for later?"

"Let's save it. I can put a couple of logs on the fire, we can put Christmas carols on, and I can give Shadow his new chew toy, too."

She laughed and it felt good. Her whole experience tonight with church and his family had been heart-catching. She saw how close this family was. Would her child be a part of this? How could she deny any child this type of togetherness?

"You've been quiet tonight," Grady murmured close to her ear. "What are you thinking?"

"I'm thinking your family doesn't realize how special they are. When I was a little girl, I would have done anything, said anything, been anything to have this kind of family—parents who hug their kids, grandparents who don't feel kids are a bother." She abruptly stopped. "Sorry. I shouldn't have let all of that spill out."

"You can let whatever you want spill out. We're friends now, aren't we?"

Was that what they were? She couldn't help but ask, "Like you and Cassidy are friends?"

"No," he admitted. "There are sparks between us that I never had with Cassidy."

As Francesca absorbed that, Patrick Fitzgerald stood and handed out the presents under the tree. She was surprised when she received gifts from Laurie, Jenna and

Maureen. After she'd left Grady that night in the saddle shop, she'd found gifts for his parents, brothers and sister. For Patrick she'd bought a book about old saddles, for Maureen a cookbook of favorite Irish recipes. She'd picked up lotions and bath products for Jenna and Laurie. John, Liam and Mark seemed to be prime candidates for treats from the candy shop. She'd had the most fun buying books for the children according to their age ranges.

When she opened Laurie's present, she discovered a delicate multicolored crocheted scarf. "It's beautiful," she told her.

"I make them in my spare time."

Francesca draped the scarf around her neck. It was perfect with her off-white sweater. "Thank you so much." Impulsively she gave Laurie a hug.

Grady's sister looked pleased and hugged her back.

Jenna's present was a small trinket box in the shape of a butterfly decorated with crystals. Francesca thanked her and gave her a hug, too.

Maureen stood by her side as Francesca unwrapped her gift. It was a mother's book, where she could record everything in her life she wanted her child to know. When she stood to give Maureen a hug, she was a little more hesitant, but Maureen wasn't.

Grady's mom gathered her in her arms and squeezed her tight. "We want you and your baby to feel at home with us. Will you remember that?"

Tears came to Francesca's eyes as she nodded. "Yes, I'll remember that."

The only one who had been standoffish all evening

was Liam. Now, as everyone disposed of wrapping paper and ribbons, as Grady went to the kitchen to refill their glasses, Liam sank down next to Francesca on the love seat. "Thanks for the candy."

"You're welcome. I hope you like cashew brittle."

"I didn't get you anything."

"Christmas isn't about that."

He gave her a quizzical look. "What do you mean? Everyone exchanged gifts."

"At Christmas you should give gifts because you want to, not because you have to."

He thought about that, then he asked, "Are you going to quit work after the baby's born and let Grady take care of you?"

She didn't know where Liam was coming from—if he was bitter because his wife had done that or if he was just trying to protect Grady. "I don't intend to quit working."

"How are you going to take care of the baby and be a doctor, too?"

"Women have families and careers these days," she pointed out to him.

He grunted. "That might work in theory."

"Grady asked me to move in with him. Did he tell you that?"

Liam's eyes narrowed. "Are you going to?"

"I don't know yet. My last relationship wasn't good for me, so I'm not rushing into anything now."

"Grady shouldn't rush into anything, either," Liam muttered.

"I know about Chicago," she said, wanting him to realize she knew how Grady had been hurt.

"Then you see we all just want to protect him. If you run off with his baby, it would tear him apart."

"I don't intend to go anywhere, not for a while anyway."

"What does that mean?" Liam asked suspiciously.

"It just means that I want my child to see more than Sagebrush. I want him to know there's a great big world out there that he can explore if he wants to."

"Mom said you were deeper than you looked."

"Excuse me?"

"Now, don't get all mad. That was a compliment. In my estimation, pretty women use their looks to get what they want. Sometimes that's all they've got, good looks. But you, you've got more than that. That's what Grady says, too."

"What else does Grady say?" Maybe she could figure out what he felt from what he'd told his brother.

"He says you're a challenge."

"He makes me sound like that wild mustang he adopted," she muttered.

Liam laughed. "I don't know about that, but Grady never has liked 'easy,' so a challenge could be a good thing."

The thing was, she *had* been easy the first night they'd met. For the first time in her life, she'd let her barriers down.

"Anyway," Liam added, "I'm sorry I didn't get you a present. So…how about if after the baby's born, I teach you how to ride? Grady says you don't know how."

"Are you patient?" she joked.

"I can be," he replied.

Whether Liam did take her riding or he didn't, she

appreciated his offer. "I'd like to learn how to ride. After the baby's born, we'll set it up."

Liam nodded, stood, turned away and then swung back to her again. "I just want you to know I think you're pretty brave taking on this family. That's not something just anyone could do." Then he went to the kitchen and picked up a fresh plate.

She wasn't brave. She was just hungering for a family of her own. But she wouldn't make the mistake of believing Grady could lead to that family if there was no trust between them. If all he was interested in was his child, how could *she* trust *him?*

After Grady lit a log in the fireplace at his ranch an hour later, he took Shadow out for a run. Francesca wandered around the living room, remembering when his house had felt like a home.

She set his present on the coffee table. The raffia ties and the green holly paper were masculine enough. She just hoped he liked it. Instead of worrying, she went to the kitchen and poured herself a glass of milk and a glass of apple cider for Grady.

Moments later, Shadow came bounding in, his master right behind him. Grady was still dressed from Christmas services in a blue cable-knit sweater with a gray turtleneck underneath, gray trousers and black boots.

He spotted the cider. "Thanks. You remembered."

She thought it was best not to reply. To her dismay, she remembered everything about Grady, everything about their time together, every conversation they'd exchanged.

"Do you want *your* present first?" he asked with a grin.

She looked under the tree and didn't see any wrapped packages.

"Oh, it's too big for under the tree," he explained, reading her thoughts. "It's in the spare room." Suddenly he crossed to her and took her hands. "Close your eyes."

"Grady…"

"Close your eyes and trust me."

Trust him—not to lead her into harm or danger or into something she couldn't handle. But at some point she had to take this leap of faith, even if they were just going to parent together.

"My eyes are closed. I promise I won't peek."

"And you're a woman who keeps your promises."

"As well as I can."

"That's the best any of us can do. Come on now, put your hand on my shoulder and follow me."

It was the oddest sensation walking down the dimly lit hall. Grady's sweater was soft, yet coarse under her hand. She could feel the straight strength of his back. If she bumped into him, their baby would touch his hip.

At the doorway to the room she didn't bump into him, but she came very close.

He turned, however, and took both of her hands in his, both the free one and the one in the cast. "Just come straight ahead," he ordered her. "There's nothing to trip over."

She could feel the floor beneath her feet and believed him. When he turned on the light, the shadows behind her eyes weren't as dense.

He said, "Okay, you can look now."

A beautiful, polished wood computer desk stood in

front of her. It was compact with a removable hutch. "Grady! Where did you—? How did you—? This is too much!"

He pulled her arms along his sides, careful not to hurt her casted one. "No, it's not too much. I wasn't going to get you something you didn't need. You said you needed a computer desk."

"But I didn't mean for you—"

"Would it make you feel better if I told you I got it on sale?"

She studied him, trying to gauge his truthfulness.

He shrugged. "It's one of those pieces of furniture that you'll be able to hand down someday."

When she looked up at Grady, she couldn't speak past the lump in her throat. He was a good man. Had she ever thought she'd meet one of those?

Finally, she managed to say, "I do appreciate your gift. I'll have a place to work now."

There was a glimmer in Grady's eyes that told her he was going to kiss her if they kept standing here. So she stepped back, grabbed his hand and said, "Now let's go see if you like *your* present."

A few moments later they'd settled on the sofa. She handed him the package and he balanced it on his lap. "Is it breakable?"

"Could be."

"Does it have moving parts?"

"Not exactly. Go on, open it."

"Anticipation is a wonderful thing," he teased.

"But anticipation isn't the real event. You've got to get past it to find that." When she glanced at Grady, she realized they weren't talking about his Christmas present any longer.

She felt her body warm in anticipation of feeling even closer to Grady. Tonight had been about family and acceptance and Christmas. Now they were left with just the two of them.

Grady untied the green raffia and slipped off the holly paper. When he lifted the lid off the box, he found two pieces of Styrofoam taped together. He separated them and discovered a handcrafted painted pony inside.

"It's beautiful," he said, noticing the artist's name on the horse. "How did you get one of hers? I heard this year's were all sold out. She only paints three hundred to sell every Christmas."

"I found it online. I noticed your collection by the fireplace the first day I was here."

"No one has ever given me one of these. The ones I've found, I've found on my own. Thank you. I like the horse painted on the horse's side. It's a freedom horse, right?"

"It's also known as a spirit horse, but yes, it represents freedom."

Carefully he set the horse on the coffee table. Then he leaned toward her. "I think a thank-you kiss is in order."

"How's that different from a regular kiss?" she joked, suddenly nervous.

"Let's try it and see." His voice was smoky with desire and she suspected he'd been waiting for this all night. To be honest with herself, she had been, too. What would Christmas Eve be without Grady's kiss?

Before tonight, Christmas hadn't seemed special. It had been a holiday that had reminded her of a longing for deep and abiding love, the respect and loyalty of someone who knew her and accepted her the way she was. Grady seemed to understand where she came from and where she wanted to go. More than that, he seemed to understand what she wanted for their child—two parents who would put that baby boy ahead of their own desires, wishes and aspirations. Would Grady be the perfect father? Could he be more?

The fire pop, pop, popped, and its hickory scent sailed on the draft. The odor of pine was strong, too. Grady's kiss brought to mind Christmas sleigh bells, favorite carols, smiles when gifts were given and received. Bows and shiny ornaments were only part of the story. Hearts ready to receive love were the other part. Could she love again? Could she accept love? Could Grady?

He was kissing her now, as if that was the only Christmas gift he wanted to give her. She touched his face, then laced her fingers in his hair.

He groaned, then pulled away, breathing hard. Recovering enough breath to speak, he said, "I want you to stay the night with me, Frannie. Will you?"

Chapter Ten

Francesca knew she shouldn't. If she did, one of two things would happen. Either she would get closer to Grady and she'd panic, wanting to run away, or tonight would show her they really had nothing but chemistry. Maybe that wouldn't be so bad. Maybe then she could just concentrate on her baby.

"Stop thinking," he commanded gently. "Do you want to stay or don't you?"

She wanted to stay. Oh, how she wanted to stay. "Grady, I don't know how pregnancy and hormones affect—"

He covered her lips with his finger. "Nod yes or no."

Gazing into his blue eyes, seeing the desire and hunger there, knowing hers matched it, she could only nod yes.

That seemed to be the signal he'd been waiting for. His hands delved into her hair, he searched her face and then his mouth devoured hers. This wasn't a slow stroll into desire. It was a diving plunge. Before Francesca knew it, she was swept away—by feelings and sensations that were heightened tonight. Because anticipation was the best fuel for passion?

All she knew was that she couldn't think very well when Grady kissed her like this. She reacted impulsively, matching his desire, stroking her tongue against his, trying to press as close to him as she could possibly get.

When the baby kicked, he felt it, chuckled and rubbed over his restless child. Then he drew her up from the sofa and swept her into his arms.

"Grady, I'm getting heavy."

"You may be ten pounds heavier. I lift bales of hay. Remember?"

She laughed. "You're comparing me to a bale of hay?"

He groaned. "I knew I wouldn't get that one by you. You know what I mean. I can carry double your weight."

Asleep on the rug by the fireplace, Shadow shook himself awake. But Grady said to him, "Stay."

That command seemed agreeable to Shadow because he settled again on the rug and closed his eyes.

Grady strode out of the living room down the hall to his bedroom.

Francesca had never been inside Grady's bedroom. Many times she'd been tempted to peek, but she hadn't.

Grady carried her through the doorway and she saw his room had a Western flavor. A four-poster, high-backed pine bed, king-size, took up its share of space. A suede throw with geometric shapes in brown and black lay over the deep brown dust ruffle. Chocolate-brown scatter rugs on the floor added soft, inviting appeal. He walked over those rugs now and carried her to stand beside the bed.

If she had any doubts at all, when he hugged her again, brought her close and said, "Frannie, don't be afraid," she realized he knew how momentous this was for her. Tonight wasn't just about the baby or their desire. It was about so much that had gone before and what could happen next if this was right.

"Do you want to undress me first or should I undress you?" he asked.

She didn't know if she was shaking because she wanted him so badly or because she was nervous, so she decided, "Let me undress you first."

"Go at it," he offered with a grin that was supposed to make her relax. Instead it just made her butterflies flutter more.

After she tunneled her fingers under his sweater and he lifted his arms, she raised it up and over his head. He tossed it and caught her for a kiss—a delicate, whimsical, let's-see-where-we-can-go kiss that curled her toes.

She reached for the turtleneck under his sweater and when it got caught on his chin, they both laughed. The moment was giving them the opportunity to be playful. And playful she was.

His kiss had been a surprise. Now she gave *him* one. She leaned into his chest, kissed above both nipples, ran her finger slowly down the center to where the hair arrowed under his belt buckle. He sucked in his stomach, and she knew she was arousing him. His body had gone taut, and he was hardly breathing. His stillness told her he was waiting for what came next, maybe trying to prepare himself for it. She didn't know what came next because she was playing this by ear.

"Do you want more?" she asked, letting her hand linger under his belt buckle.

"Of course I want more! But I won't let you have all the fun." With one quick motion he pulled her sweater up and over her head, quickly, yet careful of her casted arm. "Your breasts *are* bigger," he said huskily, appreciating them with his hands. His fingers spread over them, circled them, rounded the nipples with his thumbs.

"I know. It's hard for me to get used to. I was always small."

"No, just right."

His words warmed her the same way his hands were warming her, heating her, lighting a fire.

A few moments later the focus was elsewhere. Sliding his hands lower, oh so slowly, he let them lay on her rounding belly. "Is he moving?"

"A little. Not so much that you can notice. It's usually around midnight when he likes to kick the hardest."

Grady laughed. "So we're going to have a night owl?"

"Apparently."

Grady bent his head to her abdomen and kissed it. Then he kissed higher, over her breasts, up to her collarbone. Nuzzling her neck, he said, "I think it's time to get into that bed."

They had each other undressed in less than five minutes. After Grady threw back the covers, she slid in. The bed was humungous. Yet when he followed her and propped himself on his side, she wanted to be right there with him, at his pillow, her body touching his, her hand nestling in his chest hair.

They kissed, hard and wet and deep.

He broke away and rasped, "The past few weeks were like torture, foreplay without any satisfaction. I've wanted you again since that first night."

And she'd wanted him. But she found she wanted him in a different way now.

Oh, gosh! She had fallen in love with him!

The breath left her body. She felt dizzy with the idea of it. Then he was kissing her again and the startling flash of insight wound itself around their passion and hid itself in her desire. Grady awakened every womanly longing and some she didn't even know she had. His hands couldn't seem to get enough of touching her. His lips and tongue brought her to new heights of awareness about the desire they shared. She was breathless with anticipation until he touched her between her thighs. Her orgasm shook her as soon as his thumb made contact with the most sensitive spot on her body.

On her side, she held on to him, feeling as if a whirlpool were spiraling her away. He held on to her for a few moments, and then lifted her leg over his hip, thrust inside her, and the spiraling began all over again. His heat made her hotter, the length of him filling her surged through her to a new height of pleasure. His thumb on her nipple sent her spinning. Grady's kiss captured the sound of his name that echoed in her heart.

When the climax was over and the last ripple of pleasure had tingled away, when she lay wrapped in his arms, she was more terrified than she'd ever been. Her feelings for Grady rocked her and she didn't know what she was going to do about them. How could she pretend this had just been a physical encounter? She suspected that's what he wanted. He'd said he'd wanted her since the first night they'd met and the past few weeks had been like foreplay.

Could she handle simply being parents with benefits while loving him...knowing his feelings were only tied up with desire and his child?

"Stop thinking," he murmured to her, and his breathing became heavy and deep.

She couldn't. Not when she was truly in love for the first time in her life. Not when the man she loved might not love her.

Three days after Christmas, Grady threw clothes into a suitcase, unsettled more than he wanted to admit. Christmas Eve with Francesca had shaken him to his core. They'd experienced sex at its finest.

Afterward, he'd been rattled. Parents with benefits was a great idea, but what did it mean?

Francesca had seemed as rattled as he was. When they'd awakened the next morning, they'd eaten breakfast and he'd taken her home—her Christmas present in the back of the truck—without talking about the night before. She'd planned to have Christmas dinner with Vince and Tessa and Emily and Jared. He'd planned to have Christmas dinner with his family. Neither of them had known what to say or do next.

Now he was going out of town and that wasn't going

to help any of it. He wanted to talk to her about custody and that was going to be damn hard.

He picked up the phone on the nightstand, staring at the bed, remembering what had happened there. He had to call her and tell her he was leaving in the morning.

She answered her cell phone on the second ring. Had she been waiting for him to call? Why hadn't he phoned her before today?

Because he didn't know if he could trust another woman. Because he didn't know if he wanted to be more than a dad. Because Francesca had pulled away from him on Christmas morning, and he knew she had her own issues to deal with.

"Hi," he said, and waited.

"Hi," she said back, without taking the conversation any further.

"I called because I have to go out of town—to Dallas."

"This is sudden."

"Yes, it is. A friend of mine from college has a ranch there. There was a fire on his property. He's thinking about selling and doesn't know if he should or not. Anyway, he asked if I'd help him figure things out."

"You're good friends?"

"Yes, we are. We see each other a few times a year, whenever we can get away. Liam is going to stay here while I'm gone to watch over the place."

"He'll take care of the horses and Shadow?"

"Yes. He's great with horses, and he and Shadow are pals." He supposed he could have asked Francesca to watch Shadow, but that hadn't occurred to him.

When she seemed to have trouble finding something

to say almost as much as he did, he admitted, "Christmas was intense for both of us. Space might be good."

"It might," she agreed.

"When I get back, I have an appointment with a lawyer about a custody agreement."

After a moment's pause, she replied, "I guess I should see a lawyer, too."

Lawyers. Was that really the way he wanted this to play out? What other choice did he have? He had to protect his rights, didn't he? And his child's.

"We could probably do this without them, but I'd like something official, something in writing."

There was another long pause. "Because you don't trust me?"

"Frannie—"

"It's okay, Grady, I understand. You want to be a father and you don't want anything to interfere with that."

She made it sound so cut-and-dried.

"How long do you think you'll be gone?" she asked.

"Probably until after New Year's."

Was she thinking about New Year's Eve? A new year? The two of them raising a child?

"Have a safe trip, Grady."

"I will. I'll let you know when I get back."

They didn't have anything else to say so he added, "Take care of yourself."

"I will. Goodbye, Grady."

He didn't like the way that sounded, yet he had no choice but to say, "Goodbye, Francesca." He hung up the phone.

His world definitely felt as if it had shifted sideways.

Maybe this trip would give him the clarity he needed. If it didn't—

He'd keep his appointment with the lawyer when he got back and make becoming a dad official.

When Francesca wasn't at work, she could distract herself from thinking about Grady now that Gina had moved in. Grady had called a few times since he'd returned from Dallas two weeks ago after he'd spent a week helping his friend. But he hadn't come over to visit and he hadn't invited her out to the ranch again. Making love with him had ended the idea that they could be parents with benefits. They *were* more. At least there was more on her part. Apparently there wasn't on Grady's.

As Francesca went to the mailbox on the porch, she felt a wash of nausea. Lunch hadn't agreed with her. A cold wind tossed against her as she retrieved the mail and stepped inside the foyer once again.

It was Saturday and Gina was home with her. Her new friend was unpacking a box of books and loading them onto a bookshelf in the living room as Francesca entered.

Suddenly she felt sharp cramping in her abdomen. She took a deep breath.

Gina studied her intently. "Are you okay?"

"I'm not sure." Crossing to the sofa, she sat, letting the letters and magazines in her hand fall into her lap. The pressure in her tummy eased.

To distract herself, she flipped through legal-size envelopes until she froze at one that was just a little thicker than the rest. A lawyer's address was in the upper left-hand corner.

She tore it open. "The day of reckoning has arrived," she murmured when she could think again.

"What?" Gina asked.

"There's a letter here from Grady's lawyer. I'm pretty sure it's a custody agreement."

"You have a lawyer now, don't you?"

"I saw one last week for a consultation. He said if I received any documents I should bring them in to him."

Deserting the box of books, Gina came over to sit beside Francesca on the sofa. She pushed her black curls away from her brow. "What does the agreement say?"

Francesca skimmed the letter and gave a cursory glance to the other papers beneath, the tight feeling in her pelvis worrying her. She read them quickly. "It's a joint custody agreement giving me physical custody. It says until the child is a year old, visits are at my discretion. But then at age one and after, Grady has visitation at least two weekends a month until the child is five. Then we'll renegotiate. It's fair, but I just—" A stronger pain gripped her middle, twisted sharply inside her. She leaned forward, now knowing exactly what was happening and afraid to admit it.

"Francesca!" Gina cried, putting her arm around her, "What's wrong?"

"I'm having contractions. I shouldn't be. It's too early!" She automatically checked her watch to time the contractions. "Can you get me my phone? It's on the kitchen counter."

Gina ran to the kitchen and brought the phone to her. Francesca dialed Jared's number. She was so grateful when he answered. "Jared, I'm in labor."

"How long between contractions?"

"About five minutes."

"Is anyone with you?"

"Gina."

"Have her drive you to the hospital. I'll meet you there. Grab a bottle of water and drink that on the way."

The tight pain in her abdomen widened out this time until she had to grit her teeth.

"Francesca, are you having another contraction?"

"Yes," she finally managed to say.

"How close?"

"That one was about four minutes."

"Call 911. Now. I don't want to take any chances."

Gina must have been able to hear Jared because she went to the landline and dialed 911.

Francesca closed her phone and tried to remain calm. She told herself their neonatal unit was the best in West Texas. As Gina explained to the dispatcher why they needed an ambulance, Francesca opened her cell phone to call Grady. She felt something wet between her legs.

This could happen much more quickly than she ever imagined. They might not be able to stop her labor. She speed-dialed Grady, not sure if she wanted him to answer or not.

He did. "Francesca?" His question seemed wary, as if he suspected she'd received the custody agreement.

She couldn't discuss that now. She couldn't think about it now. "I'm in labor. I don't know if we can stop it. The baby's too early—" Her voice cracked.

"Where are you?" he asked in a clipped voice.

"Home. Gina called an ambulance."

"What can I do?"

Hold her in his arms. But she answered reasonably, "There's nothing you can do. If you want to come to the hospital, I'll make sure Jared keeps you updated."

"Updated, hell!"

She heard noises—horses whinnying...a door slamming. "Tell Madison I want to be in with you. Don't you need a coach?"

"Emily is going to coach me."

"Well, she can move over and give me a quick course."

There was more than one reason she didn't want Grady in that delivery room. "Grady, because the baby will be premature, there could be problems."

He went quiet and she heard the crunch of tires on gravel. "We'll deal with whatever happens."

She was grateful for his support. The distance between them didn't feel quite as cavernous.

But then he asked, "I *am* this baby's father, aren't I, Francesca? The baby is actually premature, isn't he? Because if—"

She hung up on him.

Grady rushed into the hospital, sick at heart. Why had he asked Francesca if he was the father? His doubts had surged again when she'd said the baby was going to be premature. But this was *Francesca,* not *Susan.* Francesca didn't lie.

Still, he didn't know what she was thinking now. His vulnerability unnerved him. He didn't know if the custody agreement was a good idea or a bad one. He didn't know anything where she and the baby were concerned. He just knew he wanted them both to be all right.

He had to stop for a pass to the maternity floor, then headed straight there. As he approached the nurses' desk he spotted Tessa pacing. She looked worried, a deep-down worried that made his gut turn over.

"Where is she?" He wanted to know.

Tessa gestured down the hall. "Emily's with her and Jared, of course. They thought it might be better if I waited out here. Jared might have to do a cesarean, depending on how it goes."

A cesarean. Jeez.

"I want to see her. I *have* to see her. I said something I shouldn't have when she called me." He started down the hall.

Tessa caught his arm, studied him for a good long moment and then said, "You can't go in there like that. You have to get suited up. Come on."

Five minutes later, Grady felt…weird. He was wearing a scrub gown, scrub shoes, a cap on his head and a mask. But he didn't care what he looked like.

Tessa escorted him to the birthing room. When she opened the door, her gaze met Emily's. She explained, "It's Grady."

Emily and Jared exchanged a look and they both nodded. However, Francesca, who was panting through a contraction, shook her head, her damp hair matted around her face.

Grady had to convince her to let him stay. He went over to the bed before anybody could say he shouldn't.

Emily moved aside and he took Francesca's hand.

Without preamble or explanations he said, "I shouldn't have asked you what I did. I know better. I *do,* Francesca."

She stopped panting, took a few normal breaths and focused on Jared. "Do a DNA test when the baby's born."

"No!" Grady protested. "I *believe* this baby's mine. Why do you think I want the custody agreement?"

"You want the custody agreement just in case. You don't trust me. You never will. I get that, Grady."

"We both need to work on trust," he determined. "But for the moment, believe me. I trust this baby is mine. Now tell me what's happening and don't leave anything out."

Francesca still seemed wary, but she nodded her assent. As Jared began to explain that they were monitoring the baby's heart rate carefully, as well as all of Francesca's vital signs and contractions, another contraction rippled through her.

She squeezed Grady's hand and pursed her lips together as her face turned red.

"Scream, for God's sake, Francesca. You're having a baby. Let it out." He couldn't imagine her trying to hide the pain, especially not from him. She'd tried to hide her pain all of her life and it was about time she let some of it go.

She gave a yelp, but it wasn't at all what Grady had advised.

Jared said to Francesca, "Look at me."

She did.

"With the next contraction, I want you to push harder than you've ever pushed. I want you to yell and scream and holler if you have to, but I want you to get this baby out."

"What's wrong?"

"Just do what I say, Francesca. Don't try to be a doctor now."

Emily, on the other side of the bed, rubbed her friend's arm. "Do what Jared says, Francesca. You know he's good."

Just then, Dr. Saxby came in the door with a team from the NIC unit.

"You're scaring me," Francesca said to all of them.

Emily pushed her friend's damp hair away from her cheek and Grady wished he could be the one to do that. But he'd messed up his chances with that for a while, maybe for a lifetime. He wasn't sure where they were headed. He just knew they all had to come out of this room in one piece.

Emily assured her, "We've assembled a team that's best for you and your baby."

Grady could see on Francesca's face when the contractions started again, and this time he moved close to her, bent down beside her and assured her, "You have the strength to do this for you and our baby. Come on, Frannie. Give the biggest yell you've ever given if you have to and push him out."

The next five minutes were hazy and traumatic. Francesca let out a yell like he never imagined she could. The baby slid into Jared's hands and at once he handed him off to the neonatologist and his team. They quickly inserted a tube down his throat, attached him to an IV and took him away in what looked like a plastic bubble.

Francesca had raised herself on her elbows, looking

after him. She seemed frantic to know what was going on. Grady heard the word *hypoglycemia*. He heard *IV glucose*. He heard *the lungs aren't fully developed*.

Then he saw Francesca's tears and he knew this had to be one of the hardest moments in a woman's life, when a baby she'd just brought into the world had to be taken away from her, and she didn't know if he'd live or die.

Grady put his arm around her, but she tensed and pulled away.

"He'll be fine," she said through her tears. "He'll be fine."

Emily crossed to Grady and clasped his elbow. "We have to deliver the placenta, Grady. Maybe you should wait outside now. I'll try to get Francesca calmed down and send her to her room. By then we might know better how the baby's doing."

"What exactly is wrong?"

"When a pregnant woman with gestational diabetes has a blood sugar spike, the baby responds to that blood sugar by producing high levels of insulin. As soon as he's born he's no longer receiving the extra glucose from the mother, so the levels of circulating insulin still in the baby can cause hypoglycemia. That's when blood sugar falls too low. Your baby requires treatment with an IV solution of glucose until the insulin and glucose levels have stabilized. He also has a breathing problem because his lungs aren't fully developed. But we're hoping over the next couple of weeks that will resolve itself, too. We have everything under control, Grady. Really. Now let us finish with Francesca, then maybe you can see her without that outfit on." Emily squeezed his arm.

When Grady's gaze met Francesca's, she looked away. Fear gripped his heart. Would their son live or die?

Chapter Eleven

Seated in a rocking chair two and a half weeks later, Francesca held her son in her arms in the Special Care Unit, so many emotions washing over her, she couldn't name them all. Those first days when a machine had breathed for Joshua Michael, she'd been filled with fear and panic. A few days ago, when he'd been upgraded from the NICU to this unit, she'd felt thankful and grateful and positively joy-filled.

Had Grady felt the same?

He'd been standing watch over Joshua since he'd been born. They'd decided on the name together. Still, she didn't know how Grady was feeling because they hadn't talked about anything other than Joshua's condition. Constant tension played between them. The question he'd asked when she'd gone into labor had created a rift she was afraid to mend.

If he kept doubting her, not only her word, but her decisions—

The doors to the Special Care Unit slid open. When she glanced up, she recognized the scrub-dressed doctor immediately.

Darren.

He passed by the other two sleeping infants in the unit along with the nurse who constantly monitored them. "How is he doing today?" Darren asked casually, as if he stopped in every day to check on the baby's progress.

"He's better, much better, and he's gaining weight. I'm hoping in another week I can take him home."

"I've checked his chart a couple of times. You and he are very lucky."

Her hormones were still all over the place and she felt her eyes growing moist. "I know we are. Thank you for the flowers you sent after Joshua was born. I haven't had time to write thank-you notes."

"You don't owe me a note."

Their eyes locked and she wondered what he thought she *did* owe him.

The doors to the unit slid open again and this time Grady strode in. He was wearing the paper protective apron as she was, and cap and mask, but his blue eyes searched hers. She knew the questions they held were a result of Darren being here.

Grady's shoulders were straight, his head held high and his stance was definitely defensive as he came to a stop beside her.

"Dr. Whitcomb?" he asked, reading the doctor's name tag.

Holding her baby in the crook of her arm, Francesca did the polite thing. "Grady Fitzgerald, this is Dr. Darren Whitcomb. He stopped in to see how Joshua was doing."

Darren held out his hand to Grady, and Grady quickly shook it.

"I'd better be going," Darren said. "If there's anything I can do, let me know."

That statement surprised Francesca and she just nodded.

After the doors slid shut again, Grady murmured to her, "Exactly what would he like to do for you?"

The look she gave Grady made him straighten. "What did he want?"

"He said he wanted to see if Joshua was okay. He said he checked his chart."

"He should stay away from you."

With her voice lowered, she responded, "He's a doctor in this hospital, Grady. I can't do anything about that."

When Joshua began to squirm in her arms, she rocked back and forth to calm him and to calm herself. "I've spoken with the chief of staff, Dr. Gutieras, and arranged for a two-month leave of absence. I also told him I'd be available for consultations. I'm hoping I can work part-time after that. That's a decision that has to go through the board."

"When will you know?"

"The next board meeting will be held in about ten days."

"Are you going to be happy working part-time?"

"I'll be happy taking care of this little guy." She rubbed her thumb over his tiny little hand, marveling at how perfect he was, marveling at how much she loved him already. He had her brown hair, but Grady's blue eyes.

She knew she had to bring up a subject she'd rather ignore. Her voice low, she ventured into territory they had to navigate. "Our lives have been in such an up-heaval since the day I went into labor that we haven't talked about the custody agreement."

Matching her hushed tone, he said, "If you want to set that aside for now, I'll understand."

She kept her gaze on Joshua, afraid too much emotion would show. "I faxed it to my lawyer a few days ago. He feels the agreement was more than fair. I signed the papers, then had them notarized. They're in my locker and I can get them before I leave."

At Grady's silence, she finally met his gaze. They studied each other as machinery beeped, as an infant began to cry, as a nurse murmured to him and he quieted.

"Those papers are just a baseline," Grady assured her. "I simply wanted to make sure you would never cut me out of Joshua's life."

"You're his father, Grady. I wouldn't!"

He quickly came around the chair, crouched down and laid his hand on her arm. "Instead of worrying about those papers, I'd like to concentrate on something else right now."

Wary, she asked, "What?"

"I suggested this once before and I want to suggest it again. Instead of going back to the Victorian, bring the baby to the ranch with me. Let's really parent together."

Her indecision and doubts must have shown on her face.

He looked pained as he said in a low voice, "Frannie, in that one crazy, upside-down moment when your labor panicked me, I said something stupid. Don't let that keep us from doing what's best for Joshua."

Was she doing that? Keeping her distance? Hurting their son? Their attitudes, what they did and didn't do, how they interacted with each other from now on, would affect how Joshua saw life.

She pulled her arm a little tighter around their baby, felt Grady's clasp on her arm, gentle but firm. She thought about what visitation would mean—Grady coming to the Victorian, her dropping the baby off at his ranch. She didn't want Joshua *ever* to feel as if she deserted him. If he was shuttled back and forth, would he feel that way? Parents parenting apart was more complicated for the child than it was for the parents.

"I'll come home with you when Joshua leaves the hospital. We'll try it for a while. But if it doesn't work out—" She hoped she wouldn't regret her decision.

"If it doesn't work out, we'll fall back on the custody agreement or try something else. This is going to be a situation in progress, Frannie. We have to be flexible if we want to make it work."

Make it work. Make parenting work. Make their lives work. Make their relationship work.

Francesca knew with stunning, heartfelt sincerity that she loved Grady. There was no doubt in her mind. But learning to live with that love without making herself too vulnerable was going to be a very difficult task.

Still, she'd never stepped away from a challenge, and she wouldn't step away from this one.

Although she wanted to spend the whole day with Joshua, she knew Grady deserved his time with him, too. "Do you want to hold him now? I have to go down to my locker, pump milk and get lunch."

"I'd like to spend some time with him."

Carefully, Francesca rose to her feet, feeling Grady's hand slip from her arm. She wrapped the blanket more snuggly around her sleeping baby and handed him to his father.

After Grady took him into his arms, he bent his head to the little boy.

That's when Francesca left. Tears swam in her eyes again. She couldn't blame them on hormones this time. She had to blame them on longings and desires of the heart that might never be satisfied.

Francesca had just switched off the ignition to her car in the hospital parking lot a week later when her cell phone rang. Fishing it from her purse's outside pocket, she checked the caller ID and smiled. "Hi, Tessa."

"Hi, yourself. I hope I'm not calling too early."

"You're not. I just arrived at the hospital. Grady's meeting me here."

"Are you ready to take your baby home?"

"You mean to Grady's ranch."

"Any chance his home could be yours?"

Francesca tried to rub the tension away from between her brows. "I don't know what's going to happen. It seemed like a good idea when Grady suggested it, but now I'm not so sure. Maybe I should just tell him it was a bad idea—"

"Don't run, Francesca."

She remained silent.

"You might have gone to Grady's ranch after you delivered Joshua if Emily and Gina and I hadn't crowded around you."

"You didn't crowd around me. You helped me stay calm and deal with Joshua's condition. You helped me get my strength back so I could be at the hospital every day."

"Grady might have been able to do those things, too. Thinking back, we might have gotten in the way."

"No. You and Emily were just being the good friends you've always been. And Gina, she's helped a lot, too."

"I like her and so does Emily. You have good taste in friends."

Francesca laughed. "Thank you very much."

"You have all the baby clothes you need?"

"I do."

"We're still going to give you a shower."

"I don't need a shower. What I need is a crystal ball."

"I've heard they're hard to come by. Instead of using a crystal ball, just look into your heart. Keep it open, okay?"

"You've turned into a romantic."

"Or an optimist."

Francesca heard an interruption on the phone.

Tessa sounded a little breathless when she said, "Natalie was climbing across the coffee table. I had to rescue her before she fell."

"Is Sean practicing with the football Santa brought him for Christmas?" When Francesca had had dinner with Tessa and Vince on Christmas Day, Sean had proudly plopped the football in her lap. It was soft and just his size.

"Vince thinks it will encourage him to strengthen his arm, and he might be right. In the process, he gets to teach his son about the game he likes."

What would Grady teach Joshua? Horse care? Baseball? The importance of family?

"I don't want to keep you," Tessa said. "I know you're anxious about getting settled in at Grady's. After you do, and when you feel like talking, call me."

"I will. I have a feeling I'm going to be sleep deprived for a while, but it doesn't matter. I'm going to learn how to be a good mother, Tessa."

"You'll do just fine. Good luck and call me if you need me."

After Francesca said goodbye, she sat a moment in silence. A new life was about to begin....

The Fitzgerald clan had left!

Francesca felt mixed emotions as she sat in the nursery at the ranch at the end of her son's first day home, holding him. Laurie, Maureen and Jenna had been at the ranch house waiting when she and Grady had arrived with their baby. They'd helped with food and changing diapers and overall support. Francesca was so very grateful. Yet right now, with Joshua at her breast, she was relieved to have a peaceful moment with him.

Although she'd heard not a sound, suddenly she

knew she wasn't alone. Grady stood at the nursery door, watching her. She felt a little self-conscious, and goodness knows, she shouldn't be. She'd made love with the man. He'd seen her naked more than once. Yet breast-feeding Joshua, feeding Grady's baby, seemed even more intimate.

"Have you taken your blood sugar recently?"

It wasn't a question she'd expected. "Yes, I have. It's normal. I'm okay, Grady. It was gestational diabetes."

He nodded and stepped into the room. "You've been feeding him about every three hours."

"He seems satisfied. He's alert when he's awake. We just have to make sure he gains weight." She'd been pumping her breast milk since he was born and that's what he'd been fed at the hospital. There was no reason to believe he wouldn't continue to do well.

"Do you believe we finally have him home?"

She didn't know if Grady had deliberately used that word or not. *Was* this her home? Or would it just be her home temporarily? She loved Grady with all her heart. But what did he feel for her? She wasn't sure living with him for the sake of their baby was a good idea. When Joshua got older, Grady might want to have a separate life. Had he even thought about that?

The day had been exciting and stressful and tiring for both of them, and she didn't want to get into that conversation now. She didn't want to face conflict before they even knew peace. She didn't want to have to open herself up and ask a man if he loved her.

As Grady came closer, she felt her body respond to his presence—every nerve came alive, every muscle almost quivered with anticipation. There was still more physical attraction between them than she knew what to do with…even after everything that had happened.

"My mother says you're a natural, that you took to breast-feeding as if Joshua wasn't your first child."

"Don't forget, I've seen many mothers learn to breast-feed over the years. I think a lot of it had to do with Joshua. He took to me." She knew there was wonder in her voice, and that's what she still felt.

Her baby had stopped sucking now and was sleeping in her arms, making little noises every once in a while. She covered her breast with her bra, then her maternity top and buttoned it.

"You know I can give you a break from his feedings during the night." Grady chuckled when she showed surprise. "Don't look so dumbfounded. You pumped milk for the hospital. You can pump it for me. I can hold a bottle."

"But you get up at 5:00 a.m.!"

"So, I'll get up a little earlier if I have to and feed him first. See what kind of hours he sets. I can take at least one of the feedings, Francesca." He was leaning over her, tenderness in his eyes for their baby.

"You would really do that?"

"I really would. This is one of the reasons I wanted you to come to the ranch. We can help each other."

"Just how am I helping you?" she asked lightly.

"Aren't you going to cook me gourmet meals?"

He said it with such a straight face, she laughed. "Won't *you* be surprised!"

"I might be," he joked back. "The advantage to having

you here is being able to see my son whenever I want. In fact, can I hold him now? Do you think he'll wake up?"

The advantage to having you here is being able to see my son whenever I want. Grady's words saddened her. She wished there was more to their relationship than that.

When Grady stooped down to her, she caught the scent of day-end aftershave. She noticed the beard stubble beginning to show on his jawline. She remembered the heat of his body, the feel of his hair, the strength of his arms. She transferred Joshua to him, her heart hurting for everything she wanted and couldn't have. As she watched Grady cradle the baby, such love for both of them overcame her that she wanted to cry. She blinked rapidly while Grady's attention was on Joshua.

"Did Laurie and Jenna and my mother make you crazy being here today?" he asked without looking up.

When they'd gotten home and Francesca had seen all the baby supplies the women had brought, Grady had asked her if she wanted him to tell them to leave. She, of course, had said no.

"I appreciated their help. But it's nice to be alone with Joshua now. I haven't really had time alone with him. Do you know what I mean?"

"I do. First he was in NICU and then in the Special Care Unit with nurses around. Even when he was transferred to the regular baby unit, there were other babies and more nurses."

She laughed. "That's what a hospital is, Grady."

"I know. That's why I don't like them."

She couldn't help but ask, "And doctors?"

For a moment his attention was all on her. "I like one particular doctor who looks ready to drop over."

"No, really, I'm okay."

He took another studying look and then nodded. "Of course you are." There was something in his tone that bothered her. Something in his tone that added that little crosshair of tension.

She sighed as she took in the nursery he had created along with Liam. A cowboy on a bronc decorated one wall. On a second, a horse stood by a white fence. The crib Grady had purchased was heavy and masculine-looking. The dresser and changing table matched. Instead of a rocking chair, he'd purchased a wooden glider chair with cushions and an ottoman.

Now as he laid Joshua in the crib, she thought about the two nurseries, the two separate houses, the two separate lives. What was living here with Grady for a while going to prove?

She made sure the baby monitor was turned on, volume up, and stood beside Grady, looking down at their son. "He's a miracle," she whispered.

"A miracle the two of us helped create."

Their gazes met. "Sleep with me tonight," he suggested.

"Grady, I can't have sex—"

"I know you can't. I'm not suggesting that. If you sleep with me, we'll hear him. We can take turns. He might awaken often tonight being in a new place."

Grady was right. They could just nudge each other. Their sleep wouldn't be interrupted quite as much. "Aren't you going to work tomorrow?"

"Yes, unless you need me here."

"No, we'll be—"

"Fine," he completed. "I know. So will I. A little caffeine goes a long way."

Should she or shouldn't she? But then she realized this wasn't a life-altering decision. They were going to get some sleep and wake up to take care of their baby.

"I'll meet you in your room," she murmured.

Only Grady's quirk of a smile indicated he approved.

He headed to his room and she quickly headed to hers and did what she'd learned to do at the hospital when she'd been working around the clock. She took a three-minute shower. After she toweled off—only a few damp tendrils curling around her face because she'd swirled her hair on top of her head to keep it dry—she chose a pink silky nightgown she hadn't worn for months. Her tummy was getting flatter with her new exercise regimen.

She couldn't keep from looking in on Joshua before she went to Grady's room. Her feet were cold, her bare shoulders chilled. It was a blustery night. She knew the old Victorian would be creaking about now. She'd called there earlier to see if Gina felt deserted. But Gina had told her she was snuggled on the sofa with a down comforter, watching TV, sipping hot chocolate. After living with her family the past few months, she was actually enjoying the quiet. Francesca knew the Victorian's quaint charm. It had captivated Gina, too.

Chilled now, enough to make goose bumps rise on her arms, Francesca hurried to Grady's room.

The door stood open. He was sitting on his side of the bed in triangle-patterned gray-and-black boxer shorts. His broad back looked sturdy and strong.

He glanced over his shoulder at her. "I knew you couldn't resist taking another peek."

She smiled. "It's called new mother syndrome. I don't think I'll ever be cured from it."

When he slid under the sheet and plump comforter, she realized she would be crawling in with him. She stood immobilized for a moment.

"Get under the covers before you freeze," he advised her. "There's a cold wind tonight."

Practical. She had to view their relationship the same way. The king-size bed was so large, they wouldn't even be touching. She went to the side opposite from him, lifted the covers and crawled in, stretching out flat on her back, staring up at the ceiling.

"Ready for me to switch off the light?"

"Sure. If we don't fall asleep quickly, we might be up again before we get forty winks."

He turned off the light.

They lay there in the darkness, a thread of moonlight shining through the window.

"I didn't hang blinds because there's no one for a couple of miles. I like to see the stars and the moon when it's bright."

The bed was in a position that they could do just that.

He reached over and felt her arm. "You're still cold."

Yes, she was, but it was an inner coldness. She didn't realize she could feel so lonely, sleeping in the same bed with someone.

"*You're* warm," she returned. "And you showered." She could smell the scent of his soap.

"So did you."

She always used the same scented body wash and shampoo. Maybe its bouquet lingered longer than she imagined. "Grady, is this as awkward for you as it is for me?"

"It doesn't have to be awkward. Come here. Let me hold you and warm you up."

It was an invitation she could decline. She knew that about Grady. He was making an offer she could accept or refuse. He might not like what she did, but he didn't react in anger. So different from the other men who had been in her life. His kindness and patience were two of the reasons she'd fallen in love with him.

Because she was in love with him, she moved toward him.

He moved toward her.

They met in the middle.

"Turn on your side," he murmured. When she did, he wrapped his arm around her. The position was intimate, too intimate for her not to realize what was happening— he was becoming aroused.

When she started to move away, he said, "Don't. It's okay. I just want to hold you."

With his breath at her ear, his arm around her middle, his body as close as if they were making love, she fell asleep and dreamed of possibilities.

Chapter Twelve

When Grady walked into his house the following evening, a feeling overcame him he'd never experienced before. There was an aroma of something cooking in the oven. Joshua was sleeping in his car carrier, which was sitting on the counter, while Francesca made a salad.

"Hi," she said with a smile. "He just fell asleep again so I'm trying to put the rest of dinner together."

All too well he remembered the feel of Francesca in his arms last night. She'd slept. *He* hadn't during the first few hours. He'd been aroused and tried to distract himself from that with thoughts of the career Joshua might choose, the colleges he might attend. But he'd still been aware of Francesca's soft body against his, her silky hair escaping its topknot on the pillow, the satin of her gown against his legs. When Joshua had cried, he'd told her to go back to sleep, and he'd gotten up and fed him a bottle, appreciating every moment of holding him.

The next time *she'd* gotten up and told *him* to go back to sleep. That time he had...until his alarm had beeped. Then he'd wanted to pull her into his arms and kiss her, but something had held him back. She could go back to the Victorian at any time and take his son with her.

So now instead of kissing Francesca, he concentrated on Joshua. "Do you want me to lay him in his crib?"

"Would you? The chicken will be ready soon. Maybe we can eat before he wakes up again."

A few minutes later in Joshua's room, Grady adjusted the baby monitor. He was standing at the crib, smoothing his baby's wispy, dark brown hair, when he heard Francesca's cell phone ring.

Her leave of absence had started, but maybe the neonatal unit already needed her for a consultation.

He stood where he was, not wanting to eavesdrop, but unable to avoid it since her voice carried down the hall. Maybe because she was surprised by the caller.

"Darren?"

Grady's heart rate stepped up its pace.

"Thank you for the offer, but I'll have to pass."

Offer for what? Grady thought.

"But why should I need to go to dinner with you just to discuss my part-time position? Right now it's hard to get away. All of my time and attention are being taken up by the baby. Whatever you need to discuss, we can do it over the phone, can't we?... Yes, Chez Marie's would be very nice, but Darren—"

Grady heard the hesitation in her voice.

"I'm living with Grady now."

There was a long pause and Grady wondered if that was on Darren's side or hers.

"I know 'living with' isn't 'married to.' But as I said, my hands are full with a new baby. I know you're close to Dr. Gutieras and of course I'd appreciate a good word from you, but I can't go to dinner with you, Darren. Our personal relationship is over. You're a great doctor and I'll consult with you, but a professional relationship is all we're going to have."

Grady heard only silence now, not even a goodbye, and he wondered what had happened. After he exited Joshua's room, he heard the sound of Francesca chopping celery on the cutting board. She was chopping very fast and looked frazzled.

He wasn't going to pretend he hadn't overheard the conversation. "That was your old boyfriend?"

The look she gave him told him he shouldn't use that terminology, even in sarcasm. "What did Whitcomb want?"

"Basically, he wanted me to go out with him." She chopped some more.

"To discuss working part-time? What does *he* have to do with it?"

"He shouldn't have anything to do with it!" she said angrily. "It's up to the board. But he knows Dr. Gutieras very well. They play golf, they go out for drinks, they play cards together, and I think he wanted to barter. If

I went out to dinner with him, he'd put in a good word for me, say that keeping me on part-time would be beneficial for the hospital."

"And if you don't go to dinner with him?"

"We didn't get that far. I reminded him we weren't going to have a personal relationship."

"So now what do you think he's going to do?"

"I don't know. I hope nothing. But if he's angry about our splitting up, if he's angrier still now that he tried to resurrect our relationship and I rebuffed him, I don't know what will happen. The worst will be that I will either have to go back full-time or lose my job. I'll deal with whatever happens. I always have." Her voice had picked up firm determination.

"But you want to work part-time, right?"

She brushed her hair from her cheek, looking beautiful…but tired. "Yes, I do. Very much."

Following his instincts now, he went to her, took the knife from her hand and put his arms around her. "You'll get the part-time position. I know you will."

He would make sure that she did. She was not going to feel pressured by Darren Whitcomb about her job. His father was on the hospital board. Grady could ask him to call his cronies who were also on the board and pave the way for Francesca's request to work part-time. This problem was solved as easy as that. But he didn't want to tell Francesca what he had planned. He wanted to make it happen first.

Holding her, he stroked his hand through her hair and wished to hell he could take her to bed. That might eliminate all the tension between them. That might lead her to tell him what she was thinking and feeling about where they were going to go from here.

Yet if the board meeting was the day after tomorrow, he'd better get out to the barn and make the call. Pulling away from her, he rubbed his thumb across her chin. "I have to go out to the barn and do some chores. Do I have a few minutes before supper?"

"Sure. I still have to cook the rice."

He should tell her he liked having her here. He should tell her supper was the least of it. But he didn't…because he didn't have the courage to think about what the most of it might be.

Francesca had just laid Joshua down for his afternoon nap—the hospital board meeting on her mind—when her cell phone rang. Her heart sped up a little as she thought the caller might be Grady. However, when she checked the caller ID, she saw the call was coming from Dr. Gutieras's private number. Was the chief of staff calling her with good news or bad news?

After hellos, he said, "I'll get right to the point. I just wanted to let you know that your part-time position was approved. You'll be receiving an official letter in the mail, but I thought you'd like to know sooner rather than later."

"Thank you, Dr. Gutieras. This means a lot. I really was afraid the board might not go for the idea."

"Well," he drawled, "the calls from Patrick Fitzgerald didn't hurt. But you already had the votes you needed."

She was puzzled. "Calls?"

"Patrick has been a member of this board for three

years now and is well liked. He's also respected, so his vote of confidence goes a long way. And as I said, I could tell by the way the wind was blowing that you already had the votes you needed."

And just why would Grady's father make the calls unless Grady had asked him to? She felt first frustration and then anger rising up inside her. She didn't want Grady interfering in her career. Was this the way he'd handle their son? Try to smooth the way and not let him make his *own* way?

After another thank-you and goodbye to the chief of staff, Francesca wandered the house, restless and upset. Maybe this had nothing to do with Grady. Maybe his father had decided on his own to make the calls on her behalf.

She was still ruminating as she prepared a pot roast and set it in the oven at a low heat. Next she checked her laptop and found her recipe for chocolate pudding. Fifteen minutes later, she was pouring it into custard cups.

The door opened and she was surprised to see Grady. "You're home early." She tried to keep her tone neutral. Was he home because he already knew the verdict from the board?

"Word has it there's going to be a wind and snow storm this afternoon. I told everybody to go home. I didn't want them driving in that."

He took off his jacket and tossed it over a kitchen chair. "Something smells good."

"Is the weather the real reason you came home early today?"

"What other reason?"

"Tell me something. Did you ask your dad to make calls to board members on my behalf?"

His guilty look was the answer. "Francesca—" he began.

"Why did you believe you could exert control over my career?"

"Don't make it sound so dramatic!" he said. "If everyone wasn't on your side and you needed a couple of votes, what was the harm? Whitcomb might have been able to hurt you by voting it down."

"It sounds as if your father could influence enough board members that that would never happen."

"It was a long shot. When I told Dad about it, he wanted to help. I don't see what the harm is, Frannie. What's the problem?"

She couldn't believe he really didn't know her yet…that he hadn't realized her independence meant everything to her. "The problem is, I didn't know what Darren was going to do and it didn't really matter. I had talked to each of those board members. They knew my reasons for wanting a part-time position, as well as insurance benefits to go with it. It was no secret that lots of mothers might like similar positions. And what if Darren had pushed against it, simply for old times' sake? He could have pushed, but I still made my point with other members. They all have equal votes."

Grady harrumphed. "He's a cardiologist. The other members are teachers, business owners, a plumber. His influence could have swayed them."

"The board is set up to have balance from the hospital and the community," she reminded him impatiently.

Grady plopped his hat on the hat shelf. "Why are you so angry?"

"I shouldn't even have to tell you."

He took her by her arm and swung her around. "Explain it to me."

She stared him straight in the eye. "I want to live my own life, Grady. I want to run my own life. I want Joshua to learn to run his. I'll take care of him, I'll support him, but I won't go over his head to affect what's going to happen to him. That's control. When I learned your father had made those calls and you had probably asked him to do it, I felt as if you were trying to take control of my life…of our child's life."

"Getting that part-time slot might not have been so easy if Whitcomb had interfered," Grady still insisted.

"I would have fought my own battle if it had come to that. I think he finally realized from our conversation that what he did or didn't do wouldn't make any difference because he and I are finished. What were you trying to do, compete with him?" She didn't get a "don't be ridiculous," and that was an insight in itself.

Grady threw up his hands in frustration. "I was just trying to help."

"Well," she protested, "help is assuring me that no matter what happens, I'll find a way to work and take care of Joshua. What you did was take control. You want control over what happens to me, how I live my life and how I raise our child!"

"You bet I want control over how you raise our child. Just wait until he learns to drive and sneaks some beer. You're going to want control like hell then."

"My son won't drink and drive." Her voice was higher and louder than she intended.

"My son won't, either, because he'll have the right values. He'll be able to come to me and trust what I tell him."

"And you don't believe he'll be able to trust what *I* tell him?"

"What you and I tell him has to match, even if you're living on one side of town and I'm on the other."

"How can they match if we don't talk about the situation first?" He hadn't discussed with her bringing his father into the mix.

Now Grady looked angry, too. He grabbed his hat down from the rack, brushed it against his thigh, and then plopped it onto his head again.

"Why didn't you trust me, Grady, to let this play out the way it should? Why didn't you trust that I'd find another job if I had to? Why didn't you trust that I would do what was right for our baby?"

"And what about *me*? What if the right thing for you is moving back to Oklahoma?"

She gazed up at him with absolute sadness. "You still believe I might take your child from you. And I have to wonder, Grady, in the dead of night, do you still wish you would have had a DNA test taken?"

"No!" he erupted. "I have no doubt Joshua is my child. But I do have doubts that you'll stay."

How *could* she stay when he didn't love her?

He lowered the brim on his Stetson. "I think we'd better shut this down before it gets nasty. I'm going out for a while."

As he grabbed his jacket and left, she wanted to call out to him. But she couldn't. Not because she was afraid of his anger. Down deep inside, she knew Grady was a different man from her father…a different man from Darren. She didn't call out because she was afraid if she did, she'd find out she loved *him* with all her heart…but that love wasn't returned.

The wind roared as Grady drove to Liam's. His brother was surprised when Grady turned up on the steps of the row house he rented.

He beckoned him to come in with a warning over his shoulder. "You shouldn't be out. The wind's already over thirty-five miles per hour. It's supposed to go to fifty…with snow. What are you doing here?"

Grady didn't soft-pedal what was going on. "Francesca's upset. I had Dad make phone calls on her behalf to the board members."

"So she could get that part-time job?"

"Dad told you?"

"Yeah, he told me. He tells me everything. He tells you everything, too. *And* John. So why was she upset? Didn't she get the job?"

Grady opened the snaps on his jacket and lowered himself to the sofa. "She got the job. But the chief of staff told her she had the number of votes she needed before Dad made those phone calls."

"Oh, that was great of him. But I still don't get it. Why is she upset?"

"I *told* Dad to make the calls. She sees that as trying to control her life."

"You didn't ask her if she wanted Dad to make the calls?" Liam's voice sounded incredulous. He didn't even give his brother time to answer as he went on, "That's psychology 101 with women, Grady. You have to ask if it's what they want before you do it. Hell, that's why my marriage broke up. I never asked. I never really even knew what she needed. What does Francesca need?"

"She needs—" Grady stopped. "She had a rough childhood."

"Abuse?" Liam asked soberly.

Grady nodded.

His brother whistled low. "Then you can't put her in a position where she thinks you're making all the decisions and ordering her around."

"I don't do that."

"I asked around about her," Liam admitted. "I learned she lived with that cardiologist at the hospital before she moved in with Tessa Rossi. A friend of mine saw him for heart palpitations. He said he's a cold SOB. He smiles, but there's nothing behind it, unless another doctor is around. So if that's what she was dealing with before—can you imagine how hard it was for her to move in with *you?*"

Snow pinged against the windows. The howl of the cold front moving in told them its force was getting stronger.

Liam was right about Francesca. She was one gutsy lady. How much courage had it taken her to tell him about the pregnancy? How much courage had it taken her the day of her accident to call him again? He knew why she'd done it. She'd done it for the sake of their child. What had she said? She'd said she wanted their son to have another parent to rely on if need be. When she'd moved in with him, he'd insisted he was doing that for their child, too. But was he? Maybe his reasons had been more selfish than he wanted to admit.

The storm raged outside. Snow swirled and veiled whatever was on the other side of it. Francesca and Joshua should not be at the ranch alone in weather like this. She probably didn't even know he had a backup generator if the electricity went out. If the electricity went out—

Grady shot up from the sofa.

"Where are you going?" Liam demanded to know.

"Back to the ranch. Francesca shouldn't be there alone."

"Wait until this blows through."

"That's the point, Liam. I don't want it to blow through with her there and me here. I need to be with her and Joshua."

"Maybe you should admit what that means," Liam suggested.

"I'm older than you. You shouldn't be giving me advice."

"Isn't that why you came?"

"Hell, no. I just came to…to sort things out."

"Are they sorted?" Liam asked with a wry smile.

Grady thought about Francesca at that ranch with snow building up, the wind blowing against the shutters, cold drafts swirling through the house. Oh, yeah, he'd sorted it out. He'd been a damn fool not to have done it before now.

The sound of the wind moaned louder than Francesca had ever heard it. Snow cascaded down, frosting tree limbs, fence lines and ground cover. Where was Grady? That truck could handle almost anything, but still—

Joshua lay at her breast, nursing. As he did and she touched his little cheek, tears ran down hers.

What had she done?

Thinking about the past few months, Francesca knew she'd fallen irrevocably in love with Grady. Fear had kept her from telling him her feelings.

Suddenly she remembered what Vince had told her. He'd said, "Watch what Grady does, rather than thinking about what he doesn't say."

At the time she'd thought he'd given her a riddle. But now she realized what Vince had meant. Everything Grady had done since he'd arrived at her hospital room had shown her how much he cared. He'd made her breakfast and lunches and dinners. He'd driven her to the hospital because she needed to be there. She'd thought all of it had been about the baby. But had it?

Could *he* possibly have deep feelings for *her,* too? Could he possibly love her?

Joshua had fallen asleep now. She wanted just to hold him in her arms and never put him down. Yet she had to prepare herself for Grady's return.

A small, scared voice inside her head asked, What if he doesn't come back tonight? Wasn't that what she was most afraid of? Hadn't she given him plenty of reason not to want to come back?

As she laid Joshua in his crib, she realized her fear of loving Grady and expressing that love to him had muddled her thinking. He was a confident man, a man who was used to getting what he wanted most of the time. Yet he never used force, never used manipulation. He might be firm sometimes, but he was also tender and gentle and kind. She'd never had a man want to protect her before. Maybe that's why it had felt so strange. Maybe that's why she'd thought protectiveness was the same thing as control. But it wasn't. There was a difference. He wanted to protect her because he cared about her. At least she hoped that was true.

After she had adjusted the monitor in Joshua's room, she started his mobile. It played a soft tune and the moaning of the wind wasn't quite as invasive.

In the living room, she started a fire in the fireplace. When the logs caught, she closed the fire screen. If Grady was out in this storm, he'd be wet and cold when he returned. She could try to call him. But did she want to tell him her innermost feelings over a crackling phone? She doubted a cell phone signal would hold in this storm.

In the cupboard she found the thermos Grady sometimes used when he went to the barn. She heated milk on the stove, stirring in hot chocolate mix. While that was warming, she made a pot of coffee in case he'd prefer that. While the coffee brewed, she poured the hot chocolate into the thermos and capped it. Not knowing what else to do, she went to the front window and stared out into the storm, hoping the man she loved was safe…hoping he'd return soon.

Grady skidded around the last curve, warning himself to slow down. He wouldn't be any good to Francesca or Joshua if he rammed his truck into a tree. The white coating of snow seemed more than the windshield wipers could handle, or the defroster. But he didn't have far to go. Another right turn and down the lane. His hands gripped the wheel tightly and he realized he was more nervous now than he'd ever been. What if Francesca had her bags packed? What if she'd already left? That thought panicked him.

Until he saw the smoke puffing out of the chimney. Until he realized a light glowed in the living room. He didn't head for the garage, but parked at the front walk. After he switched off the ignition and lights, he jumped out of the truck. Then he ran up the walk and threw open the door.

Francesca was standing in the dining room at the window. When she turned to him, he could see she'd been crying. Damn, he was an idiot! An absolute idiot.

She started toward him. "Grady, I'm sorry."

"Don't," he said, tossing his hat onto the table. "Don't apologize. I was wrong to do what I did, especially without discussing the situation with you first. I *was* trying to control what happened. I didn't want Whitcomb doing any favors for you, or making your life any more difficult. I didn't want you to have to look for another job. I wanted you to depend on me to take care of Joshua while you worked part-time. What I did was all about what *I* wanted. That was wrong. I should have stopped to consider how you would see what I was doing."

She looked as if she wanted to touch him, but she didn't. She looked shy and vulnerable as she shook her head. "You weren't wrong. *I* was wrong for reacting so strongly when you and your dad were just trying to help. Grady, I've been holding something back for a while now."

His heart practically stopped. Was she going to tell him she was moving back to the Victorian?

"I love you, Grady. I've been afraid to think it, let alone say it."

It took a few moments for her words to register. But they did, and downright joy filled him.

He folded her into his arms and pulled her close. "You took the words right out of my mouth. I went to Liam for some sympathy. Instead, he told me things I needed to hear. And when he did, I realized I was jealous of Whitcomb. I didn't want him anywhere near you. Every time I'm in the same room with you, all I can think about is kissing you. I thought I was just fighting physical attraction, but I was fighting caring about you more. I love you, Francesca Talbot. I'm going to love you until my dying day."

"You love me? You really do?"

She sounded so surprised, so in awe of the idea. He knew he had to make her believe him. He dropped down on one knee in front of her, took her hand and brought her fingertips to his lips. She was crying again, but he could see this time they were happy tears.

He was feeling a little choked up himself, but somehow he had to get the words out. "I don't have a ring yet. I guess the two of us will just have to go shopping. But with or without the ring, I'm going to ask you the question. Frannie, will you marry me?"

Surprising him, she dropped down on the floor with him and wrapped her arms around his neck. Kneeling in front of him, she assured him quite solemnly, "I'll marry you, Grady Fitzgerald, whenever, wherever and however."

He laughed, covered her mouth with his and lit their passion with a never-ending fire he knew would last a lifetime.

Epilogue

April

"Where's Joshua?" Francesca asked, swinging away from the mirror, her satin-and-lace ivory gown twirling around her.

"Tell me when you're going to move!" Tessa scolded her.

Grady's mother adjusted the tulle and lace that spilled from the hat on Francesca's head. "Laurie has Joshua now. He's fine. You've got to let him out of your sight sometimes so he grows up big and strong," Maureen kidded.

Francesca laughed and relaxed. This was her wedding day and there was so much to think about. She was protective of her son, and Grady was, too. Grady. She'd be his wife soon. His wife. Reflexively, her eyes dropped to the ring on her finger, an antique setting in white gold with a princess-cut diamond. Soon there would be a wedding band below it.

"Don't get teary-eyed on us," Emily advised her, "or we'll all start crying."

Gina, dressed in teal chiffon like the other bridesmaids, handed Francesca her bouquet of pink and yellow roses. "Are you ready?"

She was more than ready. She'd never been this happy before. She could feel her love for Grady and his for her growing stronger every day. They understood where they'd both come from and where they were going. They both knew what a gift their son was and how their love for him, as well as each other, bound them together.

Francesca hugged Tessa, then Emily and Gina and Maureen. Grady's mom was fast becoming the mother she'd never had, Patrick Fitzgerald a surrogate father. Laurie and Jenna were like sisters now, and John and Liam brothers.

There was a knock on the door and Jenna poked her head inside. She was handling the guest book and making sure everything in the social hall went smoothly for the reception. "The music's about to begin. Mom, John's ready to escort you to your pew." Then Jenna disappeared and Maureen slipped out the door.

Francesca took a deep breath, looked at her bridesmaids and then said, "Let's do this."

The music began playing as Grady's mother was escorted by John to the front of the church.

Patrick was waiting for Francesca and offered her his arm. "I'm honored that you asked me to walk you down the aisle. You know that, don't you?"

She nodded and tucked her hand around his elbow.

Emily began the procession and Gina followed. Tessa, Francesca's matron of honor, went last.

And then it was Francesca's turn.

Patrick guided her with an easy stride that enabled her to see the smiles on their guests' faces. There was Vince, with Natalie and Sean, Jared with his and Emily's twin daughters, Amy and Courtney. Liam, who had been one of the groomsmen, gave her a quick salute with a grin. He visited her and Grady at the ranch often and they were becoming friends. He'd kept his promise and given her a few riding lessons. John and Jenna, along with Laurie and Mark, sat with their children.

For a moment Francesca panicked. Where was Joshua?

But then she heard her name and she looked straight ahead. Grady was standing at the altar, their baby in his arms.

"That's my boy," Patrick said proudly.

"That's my husband-to-be," Francesca murmured back.

When they reached the altar, Grady handed Joshua to his father. Patrick kissed Francesca on the cheek, and then went to the first pew to stand beside his wife.

Grady, in a black Western-cut tuxedo and without his Stetson, took her hand in his. "I love you."

"I love you, too," she whispered back. "I'm afraid if I blink, you'll disappear."

"Go ahead and blink. I'm not going anywhere."

* * * * *

Watch for books 4, 5 and 6 in Karen Rose Smith's
THE BABY EXPERTS *miniseries*
from Silhouette Special Edition® in 2010.

of pure reading pleasure

We'll be spotlighting a different series
every month throughout 2009
to celebrate our 60th anniversary.

Look for Silhouette® Nocturne™ in October!

Travel through time to experience tales
that reach the boundaries of life and death.
Bestselling authors Lindsay McKenna, Cindy
Dees, P.C. Cast and Merline Lovelace join
together in a brand-new, four-book
Time Raiders miniseries.

TIME RAIDERS

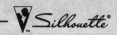

SPECIAL EDITION

FROM *NEW YORK TIMES* BESTSELLING AUTHOR

SUSAN MALLERY

DESERT ROGUES

THE SHEIK AND THE BOUGHT BRIDE

Victoria McCallan works in Prince Kateb's palace.
When Victoria's gambling father is caught cheating
at cards with the prince, Victoria saves her father from
going to jail by being Kateb's mistress for six months.
But the darkly handsome desert sheik isn't as harsh as
Victoria thinks he is, and Kateb finds himself attracted to
his new mistress. But Kateb has already loved and lost
once—is he willing to give love another try?

Available in October wherever books are sold.

REQUEST YOUR FREE BOOKS!

2 FREE NOVELS PLUS 2 FREE GIFTS!

SPECIAL EDITION®

Life, Love and Family!

YES! Please send me 2 FREE Silhouette Special Edition® novels and my 2 FREE gifts (gifts are worth about $10). After receiving them, if I don't wish to receive any more books, I can return the shipping statement marked "cancel." If I don't cancel, I will receive 6 brand-new novels every month and be billed just $4.24 per book in the U.S. or $4.99 per book in Canada. That's a savings of at least 15% off the cover price! It's quite a bargain! Shipping and handling is just 50¢ per book.* I understand that accepting the 2 free books and gifts places me under no obligation to buy anything. I can always return a shipment and cancel at any time. Even if I never buy another book from Silhouette, the two free books and gifts are mine to keep forever.

235 SDN EYN4 335 SDN EYPG

Name	(PLEASE PRINT)
Address	Apt. #
City	State/Prov.	Zip/Postal Code

Signature (if under 18, a parent or guardian must sign)

Mail to the **Silhouette Reader Service:**
IN U.S.A.: P.O. Box 1867, Buffalo, NY 14240-1867
IN CANADA: P.O. Box 609, Fort Erie, Ontario L2A 5X3

Not valid to current subscribers of Silhouette Special Edition books.

**Want to try two free books from another line?
Call 1-800-873-8635 or visit www.morefreebooks.com.**

* Terms and prices subject to change without notice. Prices do not include applicable taxes. Sales tax applicable in N.Y. Canadian residents will be charged applicable provincial taxes and GST. Offer not valid in Quebec. This offer is limited to one order per household. All orders subject to approval. Credit or debit balances in a customer's account(s) may be offset by any other outstanding balance owed by or to the customer. Please allow 4 to 6 weeks for delivery. Offer available while quantities last.

Your Privacy: Silhouette is committed to protecting your privacy. Our Privacy Policy is available online at www.eHarlequin.com or upon request from the Reader Service. From time to time we make our lists of customers available to reputable third parties who may have a product or service of interest to you. If you would prefer we not share your name and address, please check here. ☐

SSE09R

COMING NEXT MONTH

Available September 29, 2009

#1999 THE SHEIK AND THE BOUGHT BRIDE —
Susan Mallery
Famous Families/Desert Rogues
Prince Kateb intended to teach gold digger Victoria McCallen a lesson—he'd make her his mistress to pay off her dad's gambling debt! Until her true colors as a tender, caring woman raised the stakes—and turned the tables on the smitten sheik!

#2000 A WEAVER BABY—Allison Leigh
Men of the Double-C Ranch
Horse trainer J. D. Clay didn't think she could get pregnant—or that wealthy businessman Jake Forrest could be a loving daddy. But Jake was about to prove her wrong, offering J.D. and their miracle baby a love to last a lifetime.

#2001 THE NANNY AND ME—Teresa Southwick
The Nanny Network
Divorce attorney Blake Decker thought *he* had trust issues—until he met Casey Thomas, the nanny he hired for his orphaned niece. Casey didn't trust men, period. But anything could happen in such close quarters—including an attraction neither could deny or resist!

#2002 ACCIDENTAL CINDERELLA—
Nancy Robards Thompson
Take the island paradise of St. Michel, stir in scandalously sexy celebrity chef Carlos Montigo and voilà, down-on-her-luck TV presenter Lindsay Preston had all the ingredients for a new lease on life. And boy, was Carlos ever a dish….

#2003 THE TEXAS CEO'S SECRET—Nicole Foster
The Foleys and the McCords
With his family's jewelry store empire on the skids, Blake McCord didn't have time to dabble in romance—especially with his brother's former fiancée, Katie Whitcomb-Salgar. Or was the heiress just what the CEO needed to unlock his secret, sensual side?

#2004 DADDY ON DEMAND—Helen R. Myers
Left to raise twin nieces by himself, millionaire Collin Masters turned to his former—somewhat disgruntled—employee, Sabrina Sinclaire. She had no choice but to accept his job offer, and soon, his offer of love gave "help wanted" a whole new meaning….

SSECNMBPA0909